River City Ebb & Flow

River City Ebb & Flow

Dr. Jas. O'Phelan's Stories from the
Wicker Basket under this Fragile Balloon

by

Jim Biedenharn

With an Introduction by
Phil Rice

CANOPIC
PUBLISHING

Canopic Publishing
389 Lincoln Ave
Woodstock, IL 60098
www.canopicpublishing.com

Book design by Phil Rice
Cover Design by Phil Rice & Georges Stratan

First edition

   p. cm.
 ISBN-13: 978-0-9971695-3-9 (alk. paper)
 ISBN-10: 0-9971695-3-2 (alk. paper)

Printed in the United States of America
54321

for Clare

Photo by Lewis Wickes Hine

A photograph of Nashville from 1910. The telegraph office pictured is approximately at the same location as the pub where Jim Biedenharn and Phil Rice would occasionally stop for a "bucket of beer" in 1986.

Introduction

Memory can be a bit tricky sometimes, but I figure it was the summer of 1986 when I first met Jim Biedenharn. For certain it was after March of that year; that's when my dad died, and I always wished they had met. That's one of the ways certain friends stand out in my mind—the ones who I wished had met Dad.

Jim was working in the accounting office of the Hyatt Hotel in downtown Nashville. I had just joined the staff as the hotel credit manager. Having worked my way through college in the motel business, I found that my bachelor's degree in English opened less doors than my experience in the lodging industry. Thus at 26 I found myself stuck and climbing in a career not of my choosing. I have no idea how Jim wound up working in that dour, windowless office, but that's where we met.

While we were outwardly quite different, we recognized something in each other. Actually, the better phrasing is "we recognized each other," as if we had known each other well in a previous time. Whether or not it intellectually makes sense, that phrase is accurate. We also became friends immediately.

Finding a spot to share an after work beer or two (or three) became a favorite way to end the day as it allowed the rush hour traffic to die down a bit before we headed home. At least, that's the way we described it. Often we would simply drive our cars to the top level of the parking garage, sit on one of the hoods and share a quart of Budweiser. This vantage point offered a magnificent view of the Nashville cityscape as well as the sprawling suburban areas in the distance. We would swap tales of life or single out an object within site and discuss the possibilities. In this way we discovered a shared ability to detect energies from previous eras, visually and spiritually. Yeah, it sounds weird, but we prefer "eccentric."

Another favorite haunt was the Hermitage Hotel across the street from the Hyatt, which was a well-preserved 19th century landmark with a charming and relaxing piano bar. The hotel was also reputed to be frequented by some of Music City's celebrity elite, but the only "star" we ever encountered was Minnesota Fats, the aging pool hustler. He was gruff and disinterested in us personally yet cordially accepted the drink we bought him.

Sometimes we hiked a few blocks in our dress shoes, ties flapping in the wind, to a Tex-Mex pub where we would buy a "bucket of beer"—six Bud longnecks stuffed into an ice-filled tin bucket. The walk from the Hyatt brought us past many historical buildings, including the famed Ryman Auditorium, which for thirty-one years had been home to the Grand Ole Opry. As a student of history, I had a scholarly knowledge of the historical Nashville, yet Jim—a native of Mississippi—had the capacity to spout out details of places and events which had eluded my studied mind. For instance, I knew the history of the Opry; Jim knew that the Ryman was named for Thomas Ryman, a 19th Century Nashville businessman who owned several saloons and a fleet of riverboats. I would later learn that Jim possessed a unique perspective on both saloons and riverboats.

That's the way many of our conversations traveled—my structured study illustrated by Jim's intuitive knowledge and natural gift for storytelling. Thus, as we walked past the Ryman Auditorium on our way for a few cold ones, I saw the former Grand Ole Opry and felt the spiritual energy of Hank Williams and Roy Acuff while Jim experienced a tabernacle from the 1890s with a balcony funded by the United Confederate Veterans.

As our friendship grew, we began to share perceptions intuitively, which is actually quite phenomal.

One cold January day in 1987 my friend Jim told me he was giving two-week's notice to the Hyatt and taking a position as a door captain at Nashville's luxurious Opryland Hotel. He had held similar positions at high-class hotels in New York City and other places. The money was good and the work was honest. Besides, he was tired of playing a coat-and-tie corporate office game that was leading to nowhere. He also said that I should come with him. He could guarantee me a job as a valet parker, which would quickly lead to a lucrative position as a doorman. Already desperate to escape a career into which I was quickly sinking beyond the point of no return, I accepted the offer.

I never expected to remain a doorman long. I wanted to write. Not long after I took the job I was accepted into the master's program of the English department at nearby Middle Tennessee State University. It was a winding path, but eventually I would find my way. Jim would stay a little longer at Opryland but would soon continue his own academic studies, ultimately receiving graduate degrees from Vanderbilt University in Nashville and Drew University in New Jersey. He had received "the call," and he answered. Jim would finish out his working years serving as an ordained Methodist minister. And, not coincidentally, we each set beer aside permanently in order to successfully traverse our respective paths.

From the moment he learned of my literary aspirations, Jim saw me as a writer, period. He believed in me. And likewise I saw him as a literary light, regardless of whatever occupation he chose along the way. Along these lines, Jim once offered a profound comment during one of our after work beer-sipping conversations—and it has popped into my mind at several crucial moments in my pursuit of 'success' as a writer. I was grumbling about the frustrations of getting my writing published. Jim listened until I paused, and then casually said, "Well Phil, you just might come to find out that, whether or not you are ever published, you are becoming a fine work of art yourself. Maybe that's what you should aim toward. *Being* a piece of art. The rest will sort itself out." And he said it as if commenting on the weather. Such wisdom cannot be bought.

Some twenty-five years after that conversation, I asked Jim to send some of his stories to me at Canopic Publishing. He was still working as a minister at the time and used the pseudonym Dr. Jas. O'Phelan to avoid any unnecessary conflict with the flock. As I read through the writings, I found myself trying to figure out if the stories were intended as memoir or fiction. Then I realized that as a writer he is combining pieces of his life with his visionary abilities. The time and place are simply provided by context. With that realization in place, I quit worrying about trying to classify the stories. Was the Ryman a tabernacle built by Confederate veterans or was it the Grand Ole Opry? The answer is yes. Are the tales of Dr. Jas. O'Phelan memoir or are they fiction? The answer is yes. And in both cases, more.

Jim Biedenharn writes in a distinctly Southern voice, a rarity in 21st century literature. Yet the reader will find neither a glorification nor a condemnation of the historical South. The author's theological awareness does not allow him to be stuck in such follies of humankind. For the characters that live in *River City Ebb & Flow: Dr. Jas. O'Phelan's Stories from the Wicker Basket under this Fragile Balloon,* human follies are only pertinent in context of redemption—or the lack thereof.

In many ways this little collection of stories just may identify Jim Biedenharn as the last genuine voice of Southern Literature. Grandiose? Maybe. But the proof is in the writing.

Phil Rice
Canopic Publishing, 2017

River City Ebb & Flow

Contents

River City Ebb and Flow

I grew up in a small town on the Mississippi River. I bonded with seven colleagues of my age living near me. We thought our neighborhood was an example of how life was everywhere. We romped and played as immature young boys thinking that our stomping ground was an example of the greater world. Gradually we became aware of the toxins in our town when we began to matriculate into our community at the age of nine, ten, and eleven; we were Likewise unaware of the state of the world until we left our town and started working. All of us discovered that the whole of this world was full of good and evil and the choice was ours to make.

Chambers Street was the neighborhood in which we grew up. It was close to downtown and was populated by all kinds of people. There were renters and homeowners; two bank presidents, a judge, a lawyer, and people just getting started in various occupations. Tall trees of oak lined the street and numerous large homes stood stately and silent. My friends and I roamed all over the area in which we lived, playing games and sports; we had large yards in which to play and twelve acres of woods behind Mrs. Johnson's house to explore. We referred to ourselves as the Chambers Street Gang. The members of our so called gang include two sets of brothers: Richard and Bill and Jerry and Frank; Ben, Sidney, Bob, and I completed the group. Bob and the Campbell brothers had lived in the neighborhood since birth. Richard, Bill, and Ben moved in about the same time that I did and Sidney came after being adopted by the family of one of the bank presidents after the horrific suicidal death of his parents.

Bob had developed something he called the Radar Fort before we knew each other. The so called fort was a wire he stretched through the Johnson woods and back to his house; it remained for years and we often tripped over it as we wandered the woods. In our fervent games and sports, we almost ruined Mrs. Johnson's yard and basically turned it into a mud puddle. Eventually we had to shift to the field behind lawyer Emmit Ward's house, which was around the corner; we called it Squirrel Stadium. Our dogs accompanied us wherever we went. Jerry and Frank had Sockey, Ben had Trouble, and I had Sissy. Like us, the dogs often broke into fights and then settled down quickly. Bob's father had two most prolific animals called Peanuts and Patsy. They bred constantly and Mr. Andrews would let Peanuts, Patsy, and the puppies out on the roof of the Andrews' home every night. The noise which the dogs created kept my little brother up past bed-time because our house was next door and his room was the closest to the dogs roaming Bob's roof.

A very large lady named Miss Clue sat on her front porch and seemed to be watching us at all times. One day we were going to Bob's house to get him to play with us. We walked past Miss Clue's house and went into Bob's yard across the street. When we entered the yard, Bob's giant rooster came after us, flapping his wings in frenzy and pecking us. We dodged the angry chicken and knocked on Bob's door; his grandmother, who was over 90 years old and senile, answered the door naked. We turned and ran for the hills unsure what was going on and turning around we saw her unclothed in the yard putting the rooster back in his cage. Miss Clue saw all from her front porch and from that day onward she watched us even more carefully.

On my tenth birthday party we arranged a contest in Miss Johnson's yard which was next to our house. The idea was that we line up and take turns trying to tackle Longhead Bob, who was much larger than any of us. The

prize was to be a balloon; I forget who was able to tackle
Bob but no one took the balloon. Later that day, Ben
threw a match into a sewer hole and caused an explosion
that rocked the neighborhood. Thinking he would be in
trouble, all of us mounted our bicycles and rode to the
waterfront hoping no one would figure out who or what
caused the explosion. Soon all was back to normal.

As we grew older we decided to have a boxing
tournament. It involved our four Catholics versus our
four Protestants. The Catholics—Richard, Bill, Jerry, and
Frank—trained at the Campbell home and Ben, Sidney,
Bob, and I trained at my house. We worked out, ran and
lifted stones for two days preparing for the battle. At our
age, we thought we were ready. The ring was set up in the
Campbell's front yard and the fights began. First in the ring
was Frank and Sidney; Frank, substantially the taller of the
two, won over a most resistant Sidney. The next match was
between Ben and Jerry. Jerry was actually a talented boxer
with quick hands and although Ben was very athletic he
went down. I stepped into the ring next to do battle with
Bill. He had cleaned my clock during a training bout and
knocked me into a flower bed with an uppercut but this
time I was able to defend myself and pop him a couple
of times. He probably could have whipped me again but I
think he got bored and when his father pulled up in his car
Bill removed his gloves and joined his dad and left.

The last bout was between Bob and Richard. Bob
was the tallest of all the boys and we often referred to
him as Longhead. He had made a boxing robe from
his bathrobe and written "Longhead Bob" on the back.
Richard was able to get to Longhead early on and had
him staggering after one round. We didn't speak to each
other for several days while we Protestants pouted and our
Catholic buddies celebrated.

A sad event that occurred later that month began to
change our view of the neighborhood. During a massive
thunderstorm one of the large oaks lining Chambers Street
cracked and fell on a passing car. All those within the
vehicle were killed. We were on the scene within minutes
and we were stunned and saddened. The family involved
was from our neighborhood. So that tragedy along
with the fact that Longhead's grandmother was running

around naked and the fact that one of our entourage had tried to sell a bottle of yellow liquid which he said was Poontang was sufficient to make us understand that our neighborhood was no different from the world in which we lived. We continued to roam and play but we were getting older and suspected that there was more to life than we had yet seen. It was time to wander the village.

In town we saw many nice folks and numerous ones of the other ilk. At our age, we focused on the bars, the clinic, and the courthouse. I must admit that at 11 and 12 years old we did not realize that most of the bars were Likewise brothels but we figured it out quickly. We had not developed religion as of yet even though our parents made us attend church, but we were not judgmental and we just enjoyed our freedom to wander all around. Often we were offered food at the various joints and as growing boys we were glad to get it; we knew workers in every joint from Goldie's to Johnny's and we enjoyed whatever food was given to us.

We were most familiar with the doctor who ran the clinic in town. We had contacts with various city officials because of our father's professions. Ben's dad was a judge; mine was a lawyer. Jerry and Frank's dad was a bank president, as was Sidney's. In addition, Richard and Bill's father worked for the government and as such he always let us know who was in town. Bob's dad was an eccentric who painted on his house every afternoon; after several years the paint was over a half inch deep in spots.

I became a most unhappy child. Nothing I did seemed to satisfy me. I loved my friends very much but I was different from them. I knew on some level that I would not be successful in the way of this world. On a Boy Scout canoe trip up in Arkansas, I was looking out of the scoutmaster's car window during a rainstorm and the news came on the radio that Mike Todd, husband of Elizabeth Taylor, had been killed in an airplane crash and I focused sadly on a rain drop that was sliding down the windowpane. It represented to me the plane going down. During the trip, my canoe mate paddled us into a bush and I was eye-to-eye with a water moccasin; fortunately neither one of us bit the other.

We grew up and after college and medical school

Ben became a physician in New Orleans and Richard became an engineer in Texas. After a tour in Nam, Bill became a police officer in Dallas. Jerry and Frank became attorneys and returned to Vicksburg. Sidney started a business in Memphis while Longhead Bob began his slow decline and I began matriculating through a series of dark tunnels in which I found myself. I had been in law school with Jerry and Frank but I had a terrible speech impediment and when called upon to review a case I could barely speak; it was not only embarrassing but it was most painful. It sounded like someone trying unsuccessfully to start a car. My journey to become like my father, whom I admired very much, ended when I left law school in failure. I secured a job in the hotel business and worked in various cities. I resided in New Orleans, Memphis, Nashville, Louisville, New York and then back to New Orleans. Somehow in these dark tunnels in which I found myself I found a deep faith in God. I began healing when I met my future wife in New Orleans; my stammer disappeared and I went to work as an office manager.

After over ten years of marriage and two children, I ceased drinking and went into treatment. My roommate in treatment would brag about how he would buy a loaf of white bread, take it out of the package, take the heels off and pour shoe polish on the bread which was placed on a glass. The color would stay in the loaf and he would drink the clear liquid which would drain into the glass under the bread. He laughingly bragged that one could read a sports page through his liver. On the night before Veterans Day, he broke out of the clinic and escaped. Having breakfast the next morning all of us in the clinic could see the tanks and jeeps and soldiers forming on the street below us for the Veterans Day parade. Most of the druggies being treated thought that the soldiers were searching for the man who had broken out. I'd had enough. After breakfast I went to the head nurse and said that I didn't even miss beer and I was not court mandated, I was wife mandated. I told the nurse that I had never had a DWI and I thought I would go back to work. She smiled and said that if I did so I would have to pay $40,000 for the treatment as insurance would be voided if I left early. I looked forlornly at the elevator door nearby which would have taken me to the front entrance and asked the nurse what we were having for lunch.

I completed treatment and several months later had a call to become a minister. My wife supported my decision. I continued working at the Opryland Hotel, went to seminary at Vanderbilt University and was assigned to a three point charge in the country west of Nashville. It was a blessing; I felt like I was at last doing what I was here to do.

We moved back to my home state after I graduated from Vanderbilt Seminary and I was assigned to a church in my home town. It was then that I found that I still was stressed about my earlier failures in life, my tenure in law school, and my speech impediment and alcoholism. The move back home reminded me of what I had sought and the turmoil it brought. I felt like I had made progress but I was not there yet. I served in my hometown for eight years, and the three churches I served were most fond of me. My wife and children were the glue that kept me together those years, for which I am grateful.

My sons graduated from high school and went to college. The next location I served was in the state capital of Jackson where my sons were attending school and playing football at Millsaps College. After four wonderful years, I was sent to the northern part of the state to a town called Byhalia. My wife had also become an ordained pastor and she was assigned to a church in a town called Independence. The church did not want a woman pastor and the stress and constant attacks caused her to decide to become a hospital chaplain. She took a job in New Orleans and I was assigned a year later to a church near there. We were happy to be together again but the church to which I was assigned was the meanest place I had ever served. Most of the people were fond of me but five people who ran the church came after me just like they had done to every pastor for twenty years. I served there four years but the stress brought me into another dark tunnel. I developed a cancerous tumor in my medial stinum; my spiritual advisor had advised me to leave and I did so.

Ironically the situation brought me much closer to the Lord. I did not bang my head against the wall asking why me; I simply asked God what I was supposed to learn from this challenge. I moved to New Orleans to be with my wife and began cancer treatment there. A doctor friend of mine, Ben, had found the tumor and got me into treatment quickly. Several months later Richard came over from Texas to play in a golf tournament with Ben and my wife and I joined them for dinner uptown. They had both been as I mentioned, very successful, and I was at the early end of a career that I had loved with the exception of my last assignment. But my friends were truly compassionate of my dilemma and my spiritual advisor told me that these periods of darkness are where we find the Lord.

After ten months of treatment, the church I had served in my hometown asked me back for a 50th anniversary celebration. My wife and I stayed at a friend's home on Fort Nogales. The day of our arrival we walked over to the fort to watch the beautiful sunset. The sun was large and orange and we could look at it directly because the light was soft. I had never seen such a beautiful sunset. We attended my former church the next day and I felt like I had changed and was not the same as when I had been there. I was much closer to God than ever and had complete trust in him. We returned to New Orleans after the services. That night I woke at 3:16 a.m. and had an epiphany; I was back on Fort Nogales facing the sinking sun and something told me that it represented my false self which was Likewise disappearing and would be replaced by the real self that God created in a new dawn. I was deeply comforted and at peace. I had reached a place that I knew I could never have reached without God. I understood now that my destination had always been to this place, not earthly glory and praise. I had finally made it to my place and I was blessed.

Such has always been the state of our world. There is nothing we can do to change it but we can change ourselves by opening our hearts to God's truth and by not judging others who have fallen into the darkness. We can change and be blessed if we so desire but the world will not be changed until the Lord returns to confront the sin, brokenness, and evil harbored in numerous hearts.

Weatherford's Horse

I pen this epistle most hurriedly; I write as one of our
species trying to make sense of this life and its fickle
winds. We owe each other nothing; your passage may have
been rougher or finer, no matter. I am willing to travel
in the wicker basket under this fragile balloon in order
to learn from my past. I know what powerful headwinds
I will face. I do so only in an attempt to give you a map
which you may choose to use or not.

You may never forget whose child you are or
from what race you have sprung. But know it makes no
difference from which land your ancestors came or which
race's blood flows in your veins. You are God's child, are
you not? Maybe you grew up in Memphis or New Orleans,
maybe you are from some Delta hamlet. Perhaps you
are European, or Chinese, or African; it is of no matter.
Hold yourselves not above or below the rest but eye to
eye with all. Since the days of antiquity the journey of
the husk in which you reside has always been the same.
The risk is yours brother; the judge awaits. You may pass
from life to death in a bucolic cart or journey to your
demise in an execution tumbrel. Perhaps you'll make your
way luxuriously seated in a closed chariot, protected from
indignities, curiosity, and hardship. Some can't be bothered;
some go insane; others grow foul and corrupt within. All

die. Is not Napoleon in the grave like the dishwasher? Is
not the headless Marie Antoinette sleeping fitfully beside
the stable boy? I only say to you that neither of us can
walk through the effluent of this broken world without
getting scum on our boots.

Surely your birth and childhood were like mine.
None of us can avoid the impact of the imprint of the
Motherent of birth, from the darkness of the womb to
the light of the sun. You may not see the indelible tattoo
that your coming imposed upon you, but upon you it
is. We are all affected by the first terrifying shock of
life's assault and we all come to knowledge of this world
through a biological triangle of man-woman-child. You
and I are shaped by our early experience no matter what
recalcitrance we offer. Such is our universal biography.

Time is rapidly passing my brother. It is time for
us to be healed. Let me tell you my story. My suspicion
is that you will find it to be much like yours. Even now
a new generation has taken the places of those whom I
remember. Familiar faces have long since passed in the
Leviathan stream. Mine is only one life, a passage round
the bend, moving into and then out of sight. My hope is
that this missive will meet with your approbation. I move
toward my hermitage. Let yourself proceed in the same
direction.

My first breath of dismay was taken in the house known
as Wisteria Hill, which was located in a small village on
the Father of Waters halfway between Memphis and New
Orleans. The world into which I was born was in flux, as
is always the case. Riches for some; famine, plague, and
oppression for others. Tyrants and bandits ravaged what
they could. Ghostly misery stalked the muddy streets. Ebb
and flow were the order of the day. Some lived on turnip
tops and refuse; others ate high on the proverbial hog. Life
was a grinding torment for some and absolute bliss for
others. I grew up among the coiled and the twisted and
the generous and kind. Such was life on the confluence of
the rivers Yazoo and Mississippi. We lived on the largest
river system outside the mighty Nile and in some ways the
flowing water all around us represented the elementary
substance of all things. Our area was a land of remarkable

of fertility, threaded by numerous creeks and rivers, semi-tropical forests and a network of lagoons.

One couldn't see the house where I was born from the road. The house was situated on the crown of the hill in a yard of patchy grass. It looked imposing at first but closer inspection revealed much needed upgrade and repair. Approach to the house was only by a rutted trail up a steep hill through a darkling copse of pine. Our visitors, and there were many, would proceed up the hill into an opening with no trees and bushes. The building in which I was born was old even then; we could trace it back many years prior to statehood. Its walls were impenetrably thick, its massive front door was studded with iron, and its windows were heavily barred. The main hallway was interrupted with a locked iron grating. The first floor consisted of parlor, music room, kitchen, and dining room; the library and study were on the second floor and various bedrooms and sleeping quarters were on the third floor. The front entrance consisted of a single stone step worn down by years of dripping rain in our semi-tropical climes; there was a sitting porch off the kitchen.

The view from our hill was impressive for this part of the country. On the east soft hills rolled toward the capital city of our state; on the north side could be seen a cemetery with dull and faded tombstones, to our south the village in which we resided, and on the west a slight shimmer of the mighty river. Our yard consisted of an area of pebbled soil surrounded by patches of dense woods. Mosquitoes bred without interference. A rail fence surrounded the two-acre yard. One little hut stood forlornly down by the back fence with a kettle to boil soap and a bench near the door beneath which our hounds, Washington and Adams, slept. A small garden and an overgrown melon patch existed beside the hut; they were most productive thanks to the ladies attending it.

I was a sturdy infant. I arrived in the chill predawn. I did not particularly want to come; my breech birth attests to that fact. But once I arrived I was bound and determined to swim upstream. With my shock of stiff dark hair and my chubby limbs, I tried to do just that. I grew and received what nourishment I could. As I began to physically matriculate my home, my first memories were of darkened faces on the rear sitting porch, teeth flashing with the burning taste of whiskey, and lighted smokes slowing mosquitoes. I vividly remember serpents crossing our yard furtively. All of us ate together in the formal dining room. Our larder was full. There was food enough on the table for all. Our cooks served the food hot and I became aware of that every time food fell into my diaper. Sometimes during the long blessings before I was put into my high-chair, I sat under the table and peered up whatever skirts were there for what reason I knew not. I was allowed quantities of cod-liver oil and allopathic medicine given in hopes of protecting me from whatever illness was afoot. The medicines worked; at least they failed to kill me. But, I was prone to asthma and developed a stutter that plagued me until adulthood.

Like you I hungered for affection and was capable of great rage; I was always demanding approval and attention. My favorite pastime was pissing off the upstairs porch and watching the arc as it fell to the ground. Perhaps foolishly, I sensed somehow that I could take advantage of a wonderful opportunity available only to me in which I would turn *prima material* into gold. My developing ego was setting out to sublimate the reality I faced into the gold that I thought I wanted. I'm convinced that my entire time on the hill was spent in sub-consciously trying to reconcile the matter of desire for what could be with what was. In retrospect it was not to be; I could not resolve the situation.

My childhood was an uneasy joining of heaven and hell. The composition of the menagerie living or involved at Wisteria Hill was most varied. My uncle, Col. C.H. Hungerford, was corpulent, but not slow. Most would have overlooked him in a line of men. He had a son who finished at Harvard and another who was no end of trouble, yet his compassion extended to both sons. He was easy to underestimate; his appearance did not belie his inner discipline. Many made the mistake of comparing him to flashier warriors, yet he was the strongest somehow. He nourished hope where most would find none; he refused to bow to disappointment and fate. He always considered ways to better the fortunes of those around him. He wore sensible boots and his uniform topcoat. He was bald and smoked a pipe; he rode a low energy animal. He was a happy man who helped all he could; I would be much indebted to him. The Oriental angels, Wu, Su and Lu, had come to Wisteria Hill when their grandparent's dry goods store had burned south of town. They had no other family near and without their grandparents, who died in the fire, they were homeless. My uncle had befriended the grandparents and invested in their store. Because of his high regard for their grandfather, Col. Hungerford felt obligated to help the granddaughters find a place to live. We offered temporary lodging and it turned into a permanent situation which was beneficial to all concerned. It was as if divine providence brought them to us.

My guardian angel was Honey Bear. He had been valet to Col. Hungerford's son at Harvard before the young man's tragic and untimely death. Honey Bear never knew when he was born and no one could tell his age. He was small and scrawny, being somewhere between 5'5" and 5'6" and weighing maybe 145 pounds. His skin was light cream colored and his hair was jet black. He was one of twelve children of Angus and Goldie. Goldie was descended from people who made their living fishing along the Yazoo and Mississippi Rivers. Angus was a stern Bible thumper who preached in backwoods churches. He was a large powerful man who scratched out a living by farming. Unlike his parents, Bear was not cut out for fishing or farming. He was able to get an uncommon amount of schooling for his day; he learned rapidly and was highly intelligent. He also played banjo and performed reels, ballads, and spirituals on his instrument. He would perform at parties and picnics for illiterate drunks where gambling and fornication were rampant. But the Honey Bear remained above it; early on he exhibited a philosophy of detachment.

The Orientals took care of the house, kitchen, and garden. Su, Lu and Tu were the sweetest companions of my childhood. The Creek warriors, Hard Face and High Hat Jim, handled the grounds and the animals while the gifted little African man, Honey Bear, personally tended to my parents and me. Each of the aforesaid persons was most loving and protective. It was a blessing and a salvation to a child broken not by my parents but by my own flaws or as my future friend Greenleaf would say by my sins in a previous life.

My father was busy with his law practice and my mother was preoccupied with other things. Both were well educated, well read, and a cut above the thin patina of culture in our Bovine society. My parents influenced me each in their own way. Dad had two sisters; one married Col. Hungerford while the other was a spinster. Dad's brother fought in the Indian war with him and subsequently was wounded and died later. My father's family had come from Germany and were confectioners by trade. Seven brothers had been involved in the business which blossomed and was most lucrative. Four of the brothers took fast horses and well-built carriages and migrated to Louisiana and Texas country to start similar business. Two of the other brothers stayed and settled on plots of land. My grandfather ran the family business; at the end he was run over by a dray cart on the river front and died from a resulting blood clot. Grandmother faded quietly and sweetly in her bedroom.

Dad worked hard at his legal practice. He was active in politics and business. When Mississippi territory achieved statehood in 1817 he was there; he became a state Senator. He traveled to Andrew Jackson's inauguration. While he was respected and well thought of by most in our village, his practice did not bring in the money his uncles had amassed. But Wisteria Hill made a good show; he was able to keep the family silver and the wolves remained at bay. In his legal practice, he exhibited a compassion for the downtrodden. He had an attractive openness that made rich and poor alike fond of him. Many days after court he would relax at the Steamboat Exchange on Levee Street and meet with future clients. He was thought by our community to be of perfect probity and high principle; he was always a gentleman in his phrasing. He went to church only one time that I remember; he was skeptical, not of God's truth but of the organized church. He was not really interested in goods and services; he lived modestly. But he splurged on my mother. He acquired a nice barouche for her, purchased rugs from New Orleans and cut glass book cases from Memphis. Thankfully he was not angry at Honey Bear and me when we accidentally rolled the new

barouche down the hill and hit a tree one afternoon while
he and my mother napped.

My Mother had been an actress; she arrived in town
on a showboat. Mother and dad were married soon after
she docked at our village. I have it on good authority that
she wept when the showboat departed upriver without
her onboard. She had met my father in Mobile during a
regional conflict. She had refused to marry him until it
became clear that he survived the war. Her reticence was
based on the fact that she had already lost one fiancé in
another war. Her family arrived in our town later that
year. Her mother and her brother traveled downriver
from Cairo during high water in a scow freighted with
pumpkins, corn, and books. Her father had been a
steamboat builder upriver in Port Fulton but died at his
desk; we were told no more. Mother did not get along
with her family. She harbored resentment about how her
father had been treated and she and her mother fought
often. Mother's family left by packet two days before I
was born and returned to Cairo. I was never to see them
again. On the surface Mother was playful. She loved to
surprise our menagerie at Wisteria Hill by pouring water
off the upper porch on to whoever stood unsuspecting
below. Her laughter would reverberate when Honey Bear
or one of the braves would run for cover. She was not
tender, nor sunshiny; life was a burden passed on to her.
Still, she possessed a tough perky stoicism; she was an
unenthusiastic Methodist. She loved bright colors and was
a wonderful painter of scenes along the river. Even a child
could sense the tension under which my mother existed.
She suffered from chronic anxiety and with obsession with
what could have been. Sunday was always the worst day;
she wept and played piano. Her sour notes reverberated
throughout Wisteria Hill.

When I came I was not a child as much as a
companion to her; my job was to ease her loneliness. We
bathed together, we went to town and lunched, we argued
over the dispensing of milk to me. She told me about
how her father was left broken by her mother; in addition,
she lamented her brother's proclivities. She was in short
my friend, not my mother. As I became more aware, my
developing image of mother did not bring a sense of

beatitude. The dichotomy between what I needed and what I got was broad and crippling. But I don't blame her; she had an upbringing much like mine. Thank goodness I had the aforementioned others to help me. I am alive and well this day because of the people I was lucky enough to have in my life. The example and the teaching offered by these people were most important to me; they gave me faith to matriculate through a broken and dangerous clime. I give thanks to Col. Hungerford, the erstwhile Honey Bear, the three oriental women and the warriors. Because of what they gave in my early years, I survived and thrived; I was able to pass the checkpoints we all face. Because of the blessings these people offered, I was not consigned to be torn apart when the mysteries of life confronted me. I will remain forever in their debt. I was basically protected during my time of innocence and vulnerability, an age when I played with the asp and stroked the lion. That I resided among the coiled and the twisted was understood to be fact by everyone but me. Unawares, I was gladly holding the asp and petting the lion while I sat beside the lamb; life at Wisteria Hill was in truth a cross section of Isaiah's biblical vision.

Hard Face and High Hat were Indians who lived on Wisteria Hill because they had been with my father in the Creek War. Father would not speak of it but the Indians told me how he ran a mighty chief off the bluff at Holy Ground. I was enthralled and wanted to know more. The braves took me into the woods behind the house and told me all. It had started with Tecumseh's brother, the prophet Tenskwatawa. He stirred up no end of trouble with a vision that an alliance between all tribes would give the Indians strength to stop further white encroachment. High Hat and Hard Face were warriors under a chief named William Weatherford, or Red Eagle, who was trying to remain neutral. Red Eagle was a mixture of Scottish and Indian blood; his father was a Scottish trader named Charles Weatherford and his mother was Sehoy. This chief thought that our government was only trying to promote safety and peace in the region and seeking to civilize the Indians by persuading them to adopt Anglo-American dress, language, and customs such as farming. Many did so but others were fearful of losing their culture and were

hostile to the changes on the horizon. Red Eagle knew
his people would be at a military disadvantage against the
Americans and he argued his points at the tribal council.
Red Eagle's tribe rejected his advice and participated in
the Battle of Burning Corn. High Hat and Hard Face
shunned the tribe and sided with the Americans. Inside
their fortress at Burning Corn Creek, the American troops
drank, played cards, and neglected precautions. The Indian
force under the prophets arrived and waited in tall grass.
The fort's gates were blocked by sand piles and could not
be closed properly. When the dinner bell rang, the war
party advanced with knives and tomahawks at the ready.
A horrible blood bath followed. My father and the two
aforementioned Indians fled by chopping a hole through
the outer picketing and fleeing to the surrounding swamp
and canebrake. They hid in a pile of logs and covered
themselves with mud. When hostile braves approached,
father and the two loyal Indians laid low in the logs and
escaped detection. They survived and High Hat and Hard
Face cast their lot with father out of gratitude.

 After the debacle at Burning Corn, Andrew
Jackson entered the war and brought an army down
from Tennessee. He promoted my father to captain and
enlisted the two loyal Indians as scouts. Jackson had Col.
Hungerford establish a supply post at Long Lake and
the deadly dance began. In early winter, Red Eagle had
recast his lot with his people. He and his tribe waited at
Holy Ground for the assault from the Americans. The
attack came and most Indians were eliminated. Chief
Weatherford was almost captured as my father's company
closed in. Mounting his horse of magnificent speed and
endurance, Weatherford galloped rapidly to the bluff
and leapt over into the swirling river. Falling many feet,
both rider and horse went under but they reappeared
downstream alive and well. Jackson gave my father a medal
for his actions. In the battle that followed soon after, the
Indians were defeated and Red Eagle, noble warrior that
he was, escaped again and rode into General Jackson's
camp at Fort Toulouse; Jackson saw Red Eagle as a great
strategist and a soldier of great courage. He became
Jackson's lifelong friend. Col. Hungerford and father
accompanied by Hard Face and High Hat returned to our

town. The Colonel retired on his military laurels. Dad and his loyal Indians resided at Wisteria Hill with us and Dad began his practice of law.

Like all who come to this earth I had to leave my humble environs and venture forth into the world at large. The community nestled at the foot of Wisteria Hill was of course my first taste of life and I was anxious to explore the community. The most important influence on our town was the river, but its influence went beyond commerce and floods. To the more astute it represented the elementary substance of all things—a vehicle for the power of God. To many of us it personified the mystery of birth and dissolution. Our river brought good and bad, life and death, and even though it gnawed at our banks constantly, it shone beautifully in the sun. Most days ships stood into port with bright paint and gold trimming, their smokestacks standing tall through the black steam which surrounded them as they came and went. The port provided for us a touch of what the interior villages of our territory did not have; the ships daily disgorged dandies, scalawags, and trollops into our midst. The little town created a symphony far beyond what most towns its size could manage. Of course, it was because of the presence of the river. We had rich folks in mansions and poor in shacks, cruelties and generosities, mud and splendor; our hamlet may have been little but it was not boring. It exhibited a strange pathos and preoccupation with death with its mixture of the brawl of the streets, the laughing song of the tavern, and the screams and giggling of daughters of joy.

But under all this noise and confusion there ran a chorus chanting to the rising God of progress. We had churches, a general store, a blacksmith shop, a hotel, saloons, a school, and a bank. We had at least three levels in our community; one along the river where houses were put up on stilts, another a little higher at the foot of the bluff and then there were the bluffs themselves. The section nearest the water was about a quarter of a mile wide with saloons and shops along the street winding down toward the docks. The second section went parallel to the river along the hills. The third section had streets winding up the bluff into the hills overlooking the river.

Nearest the river stood shanties with earthen floors and heavy curtains instead of doors; up the bluff were nicer houses. No matter where one went or resided, mud was ever present and stubborn. All the streets and lanes were just mud, black as tar and deep in most places. Hogs, as was their way, loafed and grunted in the mud daily.

Our citizens were the self-sufficing, self-supporting agrarian type. Many of the farmers were good businessmen and they planned and built prosperous farms and businesses. They systematically cleared and put into cultivation tracts of land while harvesting the timber. Outside town a smoky haze continually hung over the grey-brown earth where stumps were burned. As we prospered the whole landscape sometimes seemed to be swimming in mud and fire. To the north of town a few small farms encroached on the primeval forest of the Delta, to the south fertile soil and larger holdings, to our east scrabble land with small farms and west of us across the river was Louisiana Purchase country. Certain families, usually with English names, constituted heredity nobility. Every river town had at least one such family who lived like royalty in mansions with every luxury money could procure. Servants ministered to them and theirs; tables abounded with rare fruits, choice game, and sparkling liquor. They enjoyed spacious verandas and grounds filled with large trees. One such man in our town even had a race track and fine blooded horses on his place.

Not many lived in such splendor but all wanted to do so. Ours become an age that cared only for gold; everyone wanted a piece of the action and furthermore thought they had an inalienable right to get it. Lust for riches became the rule of life. Yet our town in spite of its rigid social structure had a certain communal gaiety. Everything we did opened with prayer. We loved circuses, revival meetings, and touring showboats. Torchlight processions and patriotic holidays were important to us. Even the folks off the larger farms, who were given to excess and reared in wealth and idleness, would come in for various events. Sometimes our town would fill with horses and numerous wagons hitched in front of stores and businesses. The horses would drink out of the troughs along the streets and stomp to keep the flies from landing upon them. All kinds of people had taken up residence with us, Chinese, Black, European, and Jewish. In these river ports, diversity was the order of the day. It should be obvious to the discerning reader that our village was decent on the surface. Yet like all towns it had both good and bad. We harbored a dangerous and dark side with the presence of alcoholism, greed, and violence. Undercurrents roiled, some of which I was about to become more fully aware.

By my twelfth summer, I had reached an age where I juxtaposed the relative safety of Wisteria Hill and its extended family with daily jaunts into our hamlet. I met Suetonius and Tatterdemalion soon after I started coming into town. Suetonius, who lived with his aunt, was the orphaned son of a Latin professor from a college in the northern part of the state who had murdered his wife and turned the gun on himself. His aunt, who lived in our village, adopted the sharp-faced little orphan. The kind woman fed, clothed, sheltered, and educated him. She forgave him the villainies of his childhood and was repaid with a life of constant anxiety and the unenduring love and gratitude of a reprobate. Tatterdemalion was the yard child of the romantic liaison of a steamboat captain, with a wife and family in Cincinnati, and a local girl of ill repute. The lovers managed to ignore Tatterdemalion from the start and he was forced to make his way on the streets. That summer of my twelfth year lazily passed. Our town for all appearances was sleeping peacefully in the humid heat. June and July were like any other summer month in our recent past but August was different.

I remember the first dawn of that August so long ago. Suetonius, Tater and I were fishing in our bateau just before daylight. Everything was perfectly still like the whole world was asleep with the exception of one cluttering bullfrog. From our boat we could see over the water a dull line that gradually became woods on the other side. A pale place in the sky appeared; then more paleness spread. The river wasn't black anymore; it became gray, and we could see each other. The mist curled up off the water and the east reddened up and we could make out the steamboats docked in town. A nice breeze came fanning from somewhere cool and fresh and sweet; but

then we smelled something rancid. In the emerging light
we noticed the carcass of a large alligator gar lying on the
sand bar near our bateau. I should have known then that
there was going to be a gleaning, that someone was going
to die, that a harvest was coming, but I didn't get it quite
yet. We rowed back to town that morning through a humid
heat that was unsettling. I couldn't help but think that
the mood of our locale was on edge. Citizens could have
roasted small briskets inside their top hats. We had become
rapacious; our balance had been upset. In this reaching and
questing for wealth and what it represented the last act of
a tragedy had begun. It would prove to be the opening step
of a most dangerous and regretful dance.

After rowing back to town, Suetonius,
Tatterdemalion, and I began our peregrinations at the
Washington Hotel. Locals and travelers opened their day
at the hotel feasting upon heaping plates of steak, oysters,
ham and eggs, grits, and whiskey. Depending on the
cook's assistant, the boys and I may or may not be offered
uneaten tidbits in the alley behind the kitchen. If Mandy
was in a good mood, she would slip us hot sugar biscuits
and figs; if she happened to be out of sorts she would run
us off with her butcher knife waving. Just being around
the hotel gave us an indication of what awaited us during
the day; what we heard would determine where we spent
our time. Discussions with regard to last night's injuries
or upcoming legal proceedings determined whether we
hurried to the landing, the clinic, or to the courthouse.
Many mornings we would notice a local businessman
sneaking out of the hotel by way of the kitchen; we knew
the forbidden fruit of which he had partaken because we
Likewise had noticed his mistress often leaving by the
front door with her hat in place and her face discretely
covered. After the hotel visit and a bite of food, we picked
our way among the large crowds of people along the
streets and the river admiring the steamboats and avoiding
the wagons slowly tumbling back and forth.

Soon we matriculated around to various joints where
drinking began in earnest around 9 a.m. Men gathered
after breakfast in long fawn colored coats and umbrella
brimmed hats, transacting their business over the various
mahogany bars. We were proud of our bars: they were all

nests of ruffians with villainous heads and gallows visages and an occasional normal business person thrown in for good measure. All four joints served as brothels with back rooms that received stolen property for a share of the profit. We could make the rounds of a morning most easily; three of the establishments were on Washington Street and one was on Levee Street near the river. Two of the bars, both owned and run by women, had dressed their haunts with little lace curtains and neat sawdust floors; the third bar had a massive steamboat wheel hanging down over the door, and the fourth had nothing to recommend it to a passing traveler except its wide doors on both sides that offered a quick escape if needed.

Often an evening's debauch would land people at our local clinic. If the walls of our ramshackle hospital could speak it would be the night cries of the wounded, fevers, childbirth, and galloping consumption. The clinic was run by a rare species of man, a doctor who divided his affections between his practice and his Bible. He had no family and he lived over his office. He did his best to patch everyone up whether or not they could pay. Many a wayward traveler passing through our town terminated their journey with the old doctor. If Diogenes had ever passed with his lantern, he might have terminated his peregrinations with the old doctor who treated rich and poor alike. Like a true philosopher, our doctor bore the inflictions of outrageous fortune stoically. He was a ruminant man and the only time we ever saw him cry was the night when a particularly viscous tornado out of Louisiana took the life of a merchant's infant son.

In addition, we saw numerous crimes and murders in our wanderings. At one bar we saw the body of a man we had observed eating breakfast at the hotel less than an hour before. His assailant walked up to him, called a name, and fired two shots. The first one missed and hit a man at the bar; the other found its mark. The frightened patrons were distraught because the killer had called the wrong name and was mistaken about the identity of the deceased. But they soon got back to their drinks and we knew we would see the perpetrator later in the courtroom up the hill. The man at the bar who had been accidentally wounded finished his drink and hurried to the clinic; he

expired three days later. Another time we saw a young
Illinois traveler with blood gushing from his breast after
being stabbed with a Bowie knife by a drunken friend
of his, and we were present when a rowdy stranger from
Tennessee threatened a widow on the street who promptly
shot him with a musket. The man was barefoot and his
clothes were ripped and bloody. He had sun bleached curls
on his head and matted blood on his wound. Violence and
conflict were common events in our community.

    Late that afternoon we rowed our skiff up to
Greenleaf's shanty boat which was moored near the
steamboat landing amid a grove of willows. Greenleaf
was an authentic seer and sage; we regularly paid visits
on him. He was a veteran of the Revolutionary War; he
had fought under Morgan in South Carolina. He spoke
in resounding Miltonian phrases. His one eye was ancient
but crystal clear. The other had been lost to the saber of
a British officer. His face was fallen like it had melted; he
was gnarled and used a hickory walking stick. In his life
he had seen and comprehended much. It was most clear
that he had taken a circuitous route to wisdom. He had
a premise that the Revolutionary War battle of Cowpens
held lessons applicable to life and that Tarleton falling to
Morgan on that field was tantamount to darkness falling to
light and furthermore proof that plumage was superfluous
and unnecessary. He kept a map of the southern theatre
of our revolution's battles on a rickety table with a Bible in
which he read only Joshua and 2nd Kings.

    Approaching the shanty, we noticed that willows
hung limp in the fading heat, sand crunched under our feet
and muddy water dripped from our shoes. The breeze was
nonexistent; a rancid stool pot was on his deck. The cabin
door hung off its hinges and a dim lamp burned inside.
Greenleaf tapped on the deck with his heavy stick. He was
hunched as if with age or weakness and he wore a tattered
old uniform. The dreadful looking old figure raised his
voice in an odd sing song and bid us to enter the cabin. We
pushed the curtains aside and entered. We offered our fish
as a gift. Without hesitation or pleasantries, he accepted
the catfish. He revealed that two people would soon be
arriving on the night packet who would change the life of
our town and my life as well. We sat spellbound, silently

wondering what changes were coming. I thought of the deceased alligator gar we had encountered earlier and now took it to be an omen.

Smoke curled over the island south of the city; the night steamer was approaching. When the fast packet made its brief night landing we could see two passengers disembark. One limped off the gangplank, the other more or less sprung. The slower one wore an ill-fitting suit of pepper and salt and a badly tied cravat. His boots were in need of polish and the wide planters that he wore were stained with sweat. The other wore calfskin boots which were tan and brightly polished with spurs-gleaming like gems. He was dressed in a black suit with tight trousers made for horseback riding. As he sprung off the gangplank, he nodded to a nearby matron and lifted his black hat daintily as if it was full of a bevy of butter flies that he did not want to disturb. The month of August had opened with minor chords and built to a crescendo. The last act of the tragedy had thus begun; it was the opening step of a dance of death. Someone was about to turn the boiler on.

Next morning at the hotel we discovered that both of last night's arrivals had quartered there overnight. One was a general from some war; the other was a malevolent actor. We watched them eat breakfast together. The general was careless in his appearance. He had an air of neglect about his person as if he had just recently finished a great exertion from which he had not yet found leisure to repair. But there was about his huge rumpled appearance a quality that induced many to instinctively trust him. The actor on the other hand appeared to be a threat to any and all concerned. He wore a small black hat, had a gold timepiece, a derringer, and a long sheathed knife stuck inside his trousers along the left side. His body was muscular and strong as if he had constant exposure to difficult toil. Seutonis, Tater, and I glanced at each other wondering how an actor could be so well built. He was dark and sullen and exhibited a fierceness mingled with a quiet threat; his countenance was likely to arrest the attention of anyone in a room with him.

Much to my surprise, when I arrived at home late

that afternoon the actor was on our sitting porch, and
his horse was being taken to the barn by Honey Bear.
I was told that the actor would be staying with us at
Wisteria Hill. He and Mother had known each other. He
was awaiting the arrival of a showboat on tour from St.
Louis heading south along the river to New Orleans. It
was expected to arrive at the end of August. He would
be practicing scenes in our music room and I was not to
bother him when he was rehearsing.

It became obvious rather quickly that the general
was on a mission. His purpose here was to recruit our male
citizens to fight in the upcoming war. He had no do doubt
whatsoever of the wisdom and importance of his stated
purpose. The old general took his daily constitutional and
ushered in a series of speeches. His speeches were given
with great pomp in which he would patriotically swell his
huge stomach, hide his palsied hands and utter poor man's
twaddle. He had a masterful plan for recruitment. After a
series of speeches he planned to stage a parade with the
famous warhorse of William Weatherford, also known as
Red Eagle, marching up the hill to the Washington Hotel
where patriotic crowds would gather in excitement and
join the troop. Accompanied by the actor, he presented
eloquent speeches on the porches of Planters Hall, Duff
Green, and Grey Oaks with zeal and enthusiasm. These
speeches focused upon love and duty towards our nation;
he emotionally laid out facts and figures about reversals
that had taken place. He spoke of the tragedy that had
befallen the nation and other political threats. The general's
dispositions sat well; he had a gift for feeling the pulse of
his audience. He wore his ornate wide brimmed hat, and
used his corncob pipe as a prop. He skillfully used his girth
and his voice. In the tried and true manner of King David,
Alexander the Great, and Joan of Arc, he had a weighty
authority and he was always performing. Everywhere the
general was received with smiles and greetings, and he
was very popular even with his blimpish figure and white
mustache. The actor was barely able to conceal his jealousy.

The old man boasted that the spirit of the country
ever rises with ill-fortune and that unexpected downfalls
can spur us to redouble our efforts. He made brief
reference to the grim reality of war but in the next breath

spoke of the life and death struggle for all we hold dearest. He told all who attended his speeches that the time had come for every man of our blood to safeguard his national inheritance. He would then tell us what steps to take to answer the call, to serve in the simplest way and to give our country the men it needs to defend itself. He inevitably closed with reference to the fact that the colossal struggle that we were waging was not for us alone; what was really at issue was the liberty of our continent and that of our people against the all-devouring tyranny of pernicious enemies gathered against us.

The results of his speeches were immediate; a shifting of the paradigm had begun in earnest. Bars were crowded and the underside of bristling mustaches sparkled with foam as they discussed his speeches. His audience loved it; the call was answered triumphantly. The rhetoric which issued forth from his mouth was at risk of awakening the rage of the savages who surrounded his various platforms. Men who were not only weak but extraordinarily stupid roared their unabashed approval. The patina of culture which spread over our society was thin enough even without the general's exhortations. The gross exhibitions of wanton stupidity by the hungover and sad of eye in the listening audience were embarrassing in retrospect; the old man had connected directly with their desire to wage war, which was exceeded only by the desire to make money.

After the series of stirring and successful speeches, Weatherford's war horse arrived. Presentation of the animal was all part and parcel of the war plan; the general had arranged for the horse to be transported up the river from New Orleans to Natchez, Vicksburg, Greenville, and then Memphis. The idea was to entice men to enlist in the coming fray. The day of the parade, the old man felt bilious and out of sorts; he stayed in his room most of the day before the parade. The actor was more than willing to stand in. I was chosen to ride the horse in the torchlight parade because Col. Hungerford and my dad had done battle against Weatherford. I found myself waiting on the stoop of the Steamboat Exchange with Mother and Dad; I wore a little military outfit that Hard Face had fixed for me. The stone stoop was still warm from the afternoon heat even though the sun had faded and the first bullfrogs of the night were croaking on Desoto Island. The wagon stopped in front of us; I heard clopping and the thud of hooves inside. We stood by while they opened the wagon door. When the animal emerged, she was excitable and solid with deep chest and sturdy legs. She pranced down the short ramp in a muscular and nimble fashion. Maybe it was better that I did not know or understand how few can ride such a horse. The man who had ridden this animal, William Weatherford, was himself a most noble warrior with moccasins exceedingly difficult and unlikely to fill. It began to dawn on me that I did not belong on this steed.

Suetonius and Tater watched enthralled from the upper window of the bar next door as Dad's freckled forearms lifted me up and put me on the animal's broad back. Her bristled hair was uncomfortable on my bare legs; my thighs were spread so far apart my hips hurt. The steed turned her head and tried to bite me on the leg with her formidable teeth. Jerking my leg back, I looked down on the men standing next to the horse and I choked as their cigar smoke wafted directly up to me. The elegant animal whinnied and stomped while slapping against some insect with her tail. I could hear the town band warming up along with the buzz of the crowd. They were restless because the heat was stifling and it had been several hours since they had gathered. The band went into a march, the signal came from the hotel window, and we prepared to go.

I took a handful of her thick mane and with Honey Bear leading the animal we started through the cheering crowd. Honey Bear turned and whispered to me, "Boy, the purpose of this parade is to get a hard up, and when that happens somebody is going to get screwed." As Honey Bear led the steed up the hill towards the Washington Hotel, three women squatted by the road and made unabashed toilet. Then they smoothed one another's skirts and brushed each other's backs. The adjacent alleys were choked with groups of men partaking of jugs of liquor. When the people saw the horse they became frenzied citizens and fervent revelers. I began to lose my humility with each cheer. My manifest self-regard increased with each step of the animal. My innate pride, much like yours, emerged from the deep fissure at my core. I straightened

41

my military cap and wondered whether the adulation was for me or the war horse or just for war itself.

In retrospect, I was engaging in classic hubris, one of the seven deadly sins and the bane of humanity. Brother, you and I are not as immune as we think. Sit on this war horse and tell me what you feel honestly. Your loins stir don't they? Don't lie! Only Christ withstood the temptation; we don't or can't. Christ resisted but you? Not a chance! The opiate takes over and flows until it conquers and the rancid illusion emerges as real and you take a backseat. Another rider takes the reigns; know it Suh! You only cling to the mane unless the almighty himself has placed you there.

As we continued up the hill from the Exchange, I looked back toward the river and noticed the flickering lamp at Greenleaf's shanty; suddenly it all made sense. I remembered a dream I had. The meaning of the dream now emerged. Somehow, I knew I had faced a battle. My dream was of hardened soldiers coming through the woods towards me while I cowered behind a low stone wall after I had laid down my weapon. Yes, it all became clear! Greenleaf's vision and the general's lies were part of what every human faces. These situations have always been and will always be; they continue as far back as one wants to go and as far into the future as man lives. The view from the horse is what we all seek; it is what we go to with no end to get. But it is of a short and febrile duration. We are seduced, we fall and then we are boiled in the caldron with the other purged crayfish. Those seductive siren calls of ambition, fame, and fortune are toxic to our fragile systems. We sleepwalk into the delusion that we are special and that we deserve more. We willingly mount these war horses and spend our lives seeking and doing battle all the while drifting, rudderless, and bitter.

I gripped the horse's mane to keep from slipping backwards off her back as we turned toward the hotel and the speaker's podium. Drinkers spilled into the street to greet the steed as Honey Bear lead us near the podium. A preacher took the reins from Honey Bear when we sidled into position in front of the Washington Hotel. We all bowed our heads while he gave a lengthy prayer about how the bloated reeking fly infested rotted corpses of our brave men were now nothing more than mounds in the earth without markers, how death poisoned the air and how we had a duty to correct the imbalance. He continued on, and on, and on; even the horse was stomping in frustration. Bored with the incessant prattle prayer, some numbskull fired his pistol in the air and the spell was broken. No one was looking anyway so I got off the horse gladly and watched the rest of the festivities with Honey Bear, Suetonius, and Tater. The actor took over; the thespian was certainly prepared for his role. He strutted all around the horse, waving his arms, now smiling, now grimacing. He spoke of the virtues of one William Weatherford or Red Eagle who was the original owner of the horse on which I had been perched. He enthralled the surging crowd, calling Red Eagle a great strategist, a soldier fit to command great armies in the same league with Washington, Napoleon, and Tamerlane. He stated in his thespian manner how Red Eagle was an esteemed leader of peace and war who was especially chosen by God. Honey Bear whispered "or the Devil" in my ear.

On and on the now unbridled actor prattled about how Red Eagle and this very horse jumped the bluff to escape. He spoke of how William Weatherford mounted this steed of magnificent speed and endurance and galloped rapidly to a point where the bluff overlooked the river and leaped with the horse to safety. The water below them coursed with great rapidity at least a hundred feet below. He came to the end and said that bounding and pitching the horse with his gallant rider fell into the river. They resurfaced downstream where the horse bravely bore him to the opposite shore. "This boy's father chased him off the cliff!" Looking at the horse and expecting to find me there upon he was taken aback, but being experienced, he held forth and got his measure of applause as he stepped back with conceited confidence.

In the meantime, the general emerged from the hotel lobby and was assisted to the platform and guided to a worn and scruffy settee that had been placed in the center of the dais for the occasion. Someone threw a blanket over the old man's shoulders; he looked worn and shaken. He trembled slightly and hoped his mind did not go suddenly blank but he was there and the crowd was delighted to see his presence. The general sat grinning at his handiwork; the glare from the torches caught a slightly golden tinge in his silken white hair yielding evidence that it had once been red. Heavy pouches protruded from beneath his eyes and deep creases ran the side of his nostrils to the ends of his lips, adding marks of age to his florid complexion. The general rose from the settee and faced the audience; he asked everyone to join him inside at a party tendered by patriotic fellows. He had engaged a private dining room and ordered meat, cheeses, and bottles of whiskey and champagne. Recruiters were present for anyone who wished to cast lots with their brave neighbors. The people surged in, shocked to find that a patriotic glutton had gotten into the reception room early and was stuffing his pie hole.

The general, apparently seeking a quiet retreat, bypassed the ballroom and went to his suite. Suetonius, Tatterdemalion, and I followed him at a distance down the musty carpeted hallway. The general entered his room. We stood on each other's shoulders and peered over the transom in an attempt to discover what was going on. The general had already undressed; we could see why he had garnered a reputation for adipose notoriety. He was propped back on bibulous pillows. He smiled benignantly on the young woman who had been awaiting him in the room. When I took my turn peering over the transom, I recognized her. She was a waitress from one of the bars. She was, shall we say, paying umbrage to the general. Spent and apprehensive, I walked out of the hotel. William Weatherford's noble steed was sleeping in his wagon. The torch light glared softly on his half open eyes; he did not acknowledge my presence. On the way back to Wisteria Hill the moon shined as a silver tunnel between the trees. Insects raged incessantly. The slope leading up to the house had a faint sheen of a patina-like silver. Our hounds ran out to greet me with their necks and noses stretched up toward me, barking and howling. I trudged the final steps to the house; home felt good and comforting even with the moon glare shadow of the dead tree standing starkly against the brick of the house.

The next morning before dawn my father rose, strapped his two big revolvers to his belt and asked Honey

Bear to bring the horse around. Quickly Dad mounted and
rode away. The night clouds were low enough to reflect the
glare of the lights of the town. From our vantage point
on Wisteria Hill we faintly heard martial music. I dressed
hurriedly and followed my father to the riverfront. I could
see in the distance the ruddy flames of the torch bearers.
At the docks, the water lay glazed, dull and surprisingly
still in the night glow. The air was chilled enough for us
to see the breath of men and horses. There were signs of
activity along the wharf; a half dozen boats were moored
to the dock. Smoking stacks and billowing steam showed
that at least two were preparing to depart. Groups of
curious idlers gathered on the water front; they gazed with
dull wonder and vulgar curiosity. Those who signed up to
join the battle to come were of varied stations in life—
veterans who had experience, ardent young men anxious
to prove their courage, fervent patriots, buffoon assassins,
and several sniveling alcoholics. Most of those coming
to board the steamer were like hound dogs in that they
had to be taken to the bush in which the bird nested and
pointed toward it. Our local cavalry was a citizen band of
irregulars, giggling boys, and planters' sons. They appeared
at a dead gallop moving through the crowd and up the
gangplank; we could hear the hooves on the planking for
several minutes.

The mounted soldiers were followed by the tumbrel
in which the general was seated. Behind him rode the
actor who wished to enliven the gloomy scene by wearing
a uniform, swinging a sabre and shouting, "there she is,
the Lilly B! She's ready to take you to war my friends!"
He leapt off the back of the general's tumbrel, swung
the borrowed saber, and shouted "On to war boys!" The
despicable thespian was proving himself to be the typical
specimen of those who lick the boots of the powerful,
always ready to flatter the successful but pitiless towards
the vanquished. He had the soul of a lackey it was true but
still he was a most talented showboat player. Church bells
began to ring. The shuffling queue of men and horses
went through the crowd and up the gangplank of the Lilly
B. I watched my father ride up the planks, ducking to avoid
a beam as he got on the deck. Honey Bear waved at me
as he walked up the gangplank; the braves, in their war

paint, walked quietly behind. I was stunned to notice the notorious rascals Dice Dickerson and Duck Decatur riding onto the ship. The thespian had not boarded; the actor's patriotism had been quenched. In fact, he was nowhere to be seen or found. The Lilly B. blew her stacks and backed out into the rolling current. They were down river and out of site within an hour. The ebullience of the morning departed almost as quickly. It was as if we had awakened from some abstraction. Then the shivering crowd was gone, shuffling up the waterfront under the sign hanging over the steamboat exchange.

The following week was filled with quiet days. The dye had been cast; most of our poltroons were gone. A few miserable loafers still hung about the town haunts but the most respectable thieves and swindlers had left on the Lilly B. Everybody had joined the army and left for glory. What locals were left in town slowly got back to their routine; soon to be widows gathered their skirts around them. An older class of deadbeats who had wholly given themselves up to hard drink stood up at the deserted mahogany bars; they were composed of eight to ten old sots, most of whom lived on Catfish Bay. They had all been in Jackson's army and some had held official positions. Notwithstanding the fact that they had wholly given themselves up to hard drink, they were still treated with a degree of respect on account of their former positions.

From the departure onward, my days were often spent on the clock tower above the courthouse looking toward the West. I could be alone up there and think of Dad, and Honey Bear, and the braves. I could review my foreboding dreams. The fever had broken but it was as if the spirits were making sibilant whispers to us.

After a week of coquettish weather, Dr. McCall and Col. Hungerford slowly came up the hill toward the house. A low energy horse of advanced age pulled the two men. The narrow wheels of the sweet reverend's old carriage jounced in the ruts. Barking excitedly, Washington and Adams raced to intercept the visitors. It was a bright soft day, a wanton morning, rife with the promise of noon heat and humidity. We awaited the arrival of the approaching carriage in the shade of the shadows of high fat clouds

that seemed to be scudding sedately above the lawn of
Wisteria Hill. The two men knocked on the massive front
door; they requested to see Mother. They were escorted to
the parlor to await her. Dr. McCall sat near the fireplace.
Standing, his stature surpassed that of his fellows; seated
he appeared reduced. His head was large, his shoulders
narrow, his arms long and dangling. His hands were small
and delicate. The pastor was thin nearly to emaciation.
His attire only served to render his awkwardness more
conspicuous. He wore a simple black coat with short and
broad skirts and a low cape; his vest was likewise black
of embossed silk cut much too full for his shape. The
vest pocket held a Bible well used. After he took his seat,
the pastor drew from his pocket and fitted to his nose a
pair of iron-rimmed spectacles. He took the Bible from
his pocket with care and veneration suited to its sacred
purposes. He crossed his boots and began to read as he
waited. While the good pastor thumbed through his Bible,
Col. Hungerford wept softly; his bald head in his hands,
and his corpulent form shuddering under his clothing.
Mother and the actor entered the parlor together; she
sat on the divan. He went to the sideboard and poured
a drink; he then sat beside her, apparently disdainful of
the intent of the visitors sitting before him. Dr. McCall
came immediately to the point. Ignoring the actor, he told
Mother that Dad had been slain and details would follow.
A blue twilight rolled in over Wisteria Hill in rich thick
waves.

There was none of the wailing and keening usually
associated with death. Our family went about their work
stoically. The girls went back to the kitchen and garden.
Mother and the actor rehearsed in the music room. I went
to the upper porch and watched the afternoon slowly go
away. The day died the way it had been born. Across the
barren acre, a warm breeze spent itself. Quilts hung lifeless
on the clothes line, smoke from an outbound packet hung
like an apostrophe over the river front. Gradually, as the
sun went down, light was reduced to feeble lakes of glow
in the sky. Night came like a gentle snake; I could see the
gas lamps being lit on Washington Street.

Early the next morning Mother and the actor caught
a steamboat for New Orleans. Weeping, she promised

she would send for me. It eventually happens to us all; the illusion of the blessed infant imbibing forever the ambrosia of the Madonna's body was gone forever. In a thrice, I had nothing—no parents, no money, no cause, no place to live. I was aware that my stressed idyll on Wisteria Hill was rapidly drawing to a close. It is the custom of children when in trouble to pass the blame and usually one's parents are given the brunt of it. I too ruminated long and hard about blaming the dad and mother. But even then I knew that fate had taken my father and that my mother had suffered her own grievous wounds. The undeniable truth was that the world in which I lived was not responding to my wants. The fact of my separation from my birth parents was a reality with which I would have to deal. Little did I know that in the end the assistance needed would be forthcoming.

Bedraggled and dejected, Bear arrived back at Wisteria Hill seven days later. Hard Face and High Hat walked slowly behind the tumbrel. They had Dad's body wrapped in a bloody quilt in the back of the wagon. I was sure that my father had been killed in some glorious battle fighting bravely with one of the devil dogs that roamed the western hemisphere in those days. Bear told me the truth; it was a case of common depravity. The murder happened while the steamboat docked on the Red River on the way to Texas. There was no battle; instead this wasted cadaverousness figure looking very little like the man I knew had lost his life in a game of five card stud. Bear told us that the troop had taken the steamer down the Mississippi River past Natchez and up the Red River to Nacogdoches. The horsemen were to disembark there and ride to catch up with the rest of the army. But they arrived after dark and had to spend one more night on board. It would prove to be a dangerous night.

Bear said, "Your father was enjoying his play with a group of gentlemen when the double-dealing murderer struck. The formidable rapscallion Dice Dickerson was playing at the table. He signaled Duck Decatur to knife your father in the back with a Bowie. The deed was carried out by Duck, who was tractable in the hands of his scheming leader." Bear continued "Your father rose grievously injured and shot his assailant with his brace of pistols. The murderous poltroon leapt in the air, uttered a piercing shriek, and fell dead on the card table. Then knowing full well who had set the deed into motion, the captain turned his pistols on Dice, who was cowering at the table and gave him last rites with his brace of pistols. Your father then walked out on deck under his own power and shook his fist at his lamentable fate and screamed, "Damn these pistoleer villains to hell." But he grew weak rather quickly with the loss of blood; the ignoble blade had pierced his innards and great and irreparable damage had been done.

Hard Face, High Hat and I helped him to his stateroom. I was with him all night; it would prove to be the room of his death. The braves guarded the cabin door continually until the end. They let no one pass. Your father continued to grow more gravely ill. He stopped speaking, occasionally he sighed. His pulse became light, breathing was torturous. His eyes became insensitive to light. The death watch began. Hard Face and High Hat came into the room with me. We stood waiting for the next breath; it came not. I peeled an eyelid back, looked closely. Hard Face listened with an ear against the captain's chest; he remained in this position for some time. The loyal Indian rose and shook his head sadly. I reached into my vest pocket and withdrew two silver coins. I placed them on Captain's eyes. It was over and done. Your father did a good job my boy. He did not focus on the sneaks who took his life. His thoughts remained clear and focused on his duties. He met his fate with resignation; we talked of his past. He spoke of you and your mother, and requested of me that I let you both know that you were on his mind until the end. The next morning the cavalry troop disembarked. The braves and I stayed onboard the steamer to accompany the mortal remains back home."

Stunned, we rose from our places and began to prepare. Dad's remains were placed on a cooling board in the music room where the actor had rehearsed. We removed the bloody quilt and placed a single white sheet over him. He had left instructions in the desk in his study which stated that he was to be buried without pomp and without ceremony. The body was not to be exposed to the nosy public. The instructions concluded that at midnight

six men were to carry him out of Wisteria Hill and to the
cemetery to the north of the house. Only one lantern was
to be used and one prayer was to be offered. We prepared
for the funeral. High Hat and Hard Face dug his grave the
next day. Su, Lu, and Wu placed a long blue army surtout
with red and buff markings on the cadaverous corpse of
my beloved father. They pinned the medal General Jackson
had awarded him to his coat. They placed his brace of
pistols in his belt and wrapped him in a fresh quilt. Bear,
Col. Hungerford, High Hat, Hard Face, Dr. McCall, and
Dad's law partner carried the coffin at midnight, six vague
figures walking through the still evening. I walked ahead
holding a flickering lantern that freckled the ground
with innumerable little spangles of light. We were under
no inspection but that of the moon and God Almighty.
Dad's grave was beside his parents, his brother, his sister,
and his nephew. Bear liberally sprinkled the quilt with
quicklime. We swiftly lowered the remains which stretched
indifferently under the quilt. Neither cross nor stone
marked the spot. Dr. McCall exhibited a decorous sorrow
when he prayed sonorously over the open grave, then High
Hat and Hard Face slowly shoveled dirt into the hole.

After the death, our lives became even more gloomy
and harsh. Events unraveled quickly. Our Chinese family
left Wisteria Hill with an equanimity which is to be envied.
The warriors returned from whence they came. Honey Bear
and I were left to fend for ourselves. But not for long. There
came a new turn of fortune's wheel. Good Col. Hungerford
contacted the shipping company in Port Fulton where my
mother's father had worked and secured positions for Bear
and me on the New Orleans to St Louis run under Capt.
Tom Morrissey on the Packet D.P. Waring. It was the offer
of a new life, an opportunity to leave behind the terrible
disorders of my childhood and embrace the exciting and
unknown future. I packed my books and my clothes. I felt
within me two currents—one taking me away, the other
linking me forever to the scene of my childhood and the
principle dwelling place of my imagination. The discomfort
and sadness that I felt would not soon fade but we had
found safe passage for now. Illusion and childhood were
over for me; all I knew was that I had to keep going at all
cost—to not quit. Nothing else would do.

The opportunity offered would prove to be a womb where I was nourished as well as could be expected. We took passage for St. Louis that night on the night packet. Suetonius and Tater stood on the cobblestones watching us get up steam; I stood on the deck waving. We pulled away from my familiar haunts. We passed Greenleaf's shanty; he sat on his porch smoking a corncob pipe. I was never to see him again. My town receded in the twilight. Honey Bear and I walked slowly to the crew's quarters hoping to get a good night's sleep.

Should someone's spade perchance break open the unmarked grave of my father, the shovel's metal may indent a hard stratum made by the slaking of lime. They may find the tarnished medal and a rusted brace of pistols. I only want them to know that the handful of pale dust which they disinter from the damp soil is the last trace of a long dead captain who in his day had been a man of grace and compassion.

Ma Brewer's Trial

In our minds the hotel, the joints, and the clinic served as a funnel to the courthouse. Located on a massive hill overlooking the river, many of the injureds' wrongs were settled in this place of justice. Much of what we were able to witness in premature form in the bustling bars came to fruition in the stark, austere courthouse. My friends Ben and Richard and I had enjoyed many a dandy dispute in the cavernous old courtroom. We had been in the gallery when pistoleers, liars, and evildoers received their just desserts.

Aside from my father, my favorite barrister was one F. W. Bergeron of Natchez. We would hurry to the courthouse whenever Lawyer Bergeron was in town to try a case. He would arrive from Natchez on a fine-blooded horse and spend the night before the trial at the Washington Hotel. He cut a strange and whimsical figure. Lawyer Bergeron was tall yet his body was unfortunately proportioned. He usually dressed in a loose coat beneath which projected his spindly legs in riding breeches and boots. A tricorn hat covered his small round head. The courtroom was his kingdom; he was an eccentric genius who was said to drink two quarts or more of Porters wine during a given day although he never seemed to be under the influence. He was noted for his acid tongue, and many feared and hated him. Politically he aligned himself with the people and against the silk stocking upper crust. When he rose to defend his clients, a crowd never failed to be drawn to the virulent abuse which he uttered in a high and piercing voice. Before entering the court house, he would put his still burning cigar in the crook of a bush near the court-house steps to be retrieved at day's end.

On this particular day in early August, the case in question was a suit brought by Ma Brewer of local fame against Colonel Hungerford's oldest son, Bugs Hunger-ford. The defense team was Frederick W. Bergeron and my father. Richard, Ben, and I were in the gallery in gleeful anticipation. The litigation alleged that Hungerford's Liv-ery Inc. had contracted to deliver Ma Brewer's just-shipped new piano from the waterfront to her place of business, which was Likewise her domicile. A careless and unscrupu-lous half breed working for Hungerford's son had under-taken to move the piano while his ne'er-do-well employer was sleeping off a frolic. The man lit his cigar, tossed his match out and accidentally set afire the tarp covering the instrument. Ma Brewer claimed that she had intended to offer lessons to the children and Likewise improve and elevate the culture of our little hamlet with the instrument. In truth, most were aware of the fact that the piano was stuffed with a large quantity of laudanum for sale and use by her customers. The tincture of opium had gone up in smoke with the piano.

The courtroom was standing room only. Most eyes were locked on Ma Brewer as she posed as an ordinary woman desiring to improve our community. In fact she was a she-wolf, the most successful madam north of New Orleans. Ma Brewer wore diamonds as large as gravel with a pendent of ruby lost among the lush billows of her breasts. Her slightest movement appeared to be accom-panied by an expenditure of breath out of all proportion to any benefit the movement could give her. She toiled down the courtroom aisle and reached the plaintiffs' table, brandishing a wooden rosary in her left hand. She wore the black silk gown in which we were accustomed to seeing her and a large hat savagely flowered. The boys and I were enthralled; we were most gleeful when she opened her purse and sipped from the small phial kept therein.

What air was moving, and it was very little, entered the open windows and crawled over the heads of the spectators. This small breeze did nothing to erase the lingering smell of tobacco and stale sweat and various musty odors. One could sense in the large courtroom the disputes and bickering which had been settled over the years. Through the open windows we could see those gathered on the courthouse lawn who had not gained admittance to the trial. Many of them were pitching gold coins back and forth between holes in the hot earth under the old pecan tree as they awaited the start of the case.

Summarily the judge was announced and the proceedings began. Judge Guider we knew to be a severe, single-minded prelate. He was considered a just man, fixed in purpose and accustomed to the pursuit of a moral obligation to the end. He had in his nature no sentimentality and carried himself in the eye of God and man with an inclement and profound devotion to duty. In addition, he was Ben's father.

Twelve jurors were drawn from all classes; a sometime farmer, a doctor, a bartender, a musician, a barber, a preacher, a janitor, a cook and four more that I can't picture now. They crowded into their box with faces already gleaming with moisture from the heat. They looked like a true cross section of our fair city; the barkeeper mused tenderly behind the rigid travesty of greasy hair and sleepy eyes. The cook seemed preoccupied; the musician was nodding off after a long night; the barber had scissors and comb in his coat pocket; the farmer had a drooped head and an open mouth with a vast, puffy face without any mark of age or thought whatever. The preacher had a majestic sweep of flesh on either side of a small blunt nose, and next to him the doctor was well-groomed and dressed nicely. Lastly in the end chair lounged the janitor, a fat man in a shapeless suit; dirty sleeves fell out of his coat and rested on his hands, which were rimmed with black nails.

The spectators within looked toward the bench with intent faces as white and pallid as the floating bellies of dead fish. They craned their necks for signs of fear and excitement in the worn yet imperturbable face of the plaintiff. But Ma sat upright and resolute awaiting the formal opening of the court. Many of Ma's customers were scattered through the courtroom. In addition, the notorious gunmen Towhead Smith, Dice Dickenson, and Duck Decatur sat behind Ma Brewer. These bravos were in her employment. Towhead was from Missouri and was dressed like a river boat gambler. He referred to himself as a professional duelist and he had a half dozen killings to his credit. He never let a soft fight pass him by. The other two men were dandied up in the finest of men's furnishings and were Likewise most dangerous.

Mrs. Brewer did not so much as look at any of the above mentioned men. She knew that she must comport herself to be the lady she imagined herself to be. Encouraged by her repeated sips of the cordial in her purse she fully intended to defend herself vigorously. The determination exhibited caused one to think that the issue in question, a burned piano made in Cincinnati, was a matter of national importance.

Ma was joined at her defense table by Mr. Dukay Volney. Volney had relieved the monotony of our fair community several weeks previously when he arrived by steamboat to research a book about the ancient mound builders. But we could tell that most of his research had taken place in Ma's back room. He lived over Ma's bar and was reputed to be one of her most loyal customers. The prosecutor, a barrister named Red Jacoby, sat next to the plaintiff and fidgeted with his papers. His vest was open over a slight paunch. He reached over and patted Ma's gloved hand and assured her that if she would be herself all would go well. Those sitting near enough to overhear this whispered comment laughed aloud. Mr. Bergeron and my father took their place as defense attorneys beside Bugs Hungerford, who appeared to be hungover.

The attorneys unsheathed their verbal rapiers and prepared for vigorous parry and thrust. The joints were well oiled now and the battle began. Lawyer Jacoby was meticulously determined to observe the outward formalities of legal procedure; he asked every question as if witnesses knew the answer to what he inquired. Witnesses answered loudly and clearly or tepidly depending on whether they wanted the answer heard or not. Jacobs hoped to garner the cost of the piano, shipping, and damages for his client; Bergeron and Dad were willing to pay for the piano and nothing else.

During the course of the morning, dialogue became acrimonious. Berger excelled at exposing the profound dissimulation wherewith the plaintiff had deceived the people of the jury. He brought out the irony underlying the proposal that a notorious madam would teach little girls of our fair and religious community to play the piano. His repeated description of Ma Brewer's perfidy had the entire courtroom in a state of riotous laughter.

When Ma Brewer took the stand in the middle of the afternoon, she watched disdainfully as Fred D. Bergeron approached the witness box. During cross examination her answers were surprisingly vigorous and at the same time cautious and shrewd. Her occupation had taught her to collect her thoughts; not for a moment did she lose her composure. Even the accusatory and mischievous questions failed to disturb her equanimity. She measured her responses and gave exact figures with regard to the cost of the instrument, the shipping, and her plans to teach the young. The cordial had taken hold of her and it was as if her responses were given not to the pettifogging lawyer before her but to the only genuine and sincere judge of all history itself. In fact, she even wiped a tear from her reptile eyes.

When Hungerford's son took the stand his replies were often ambiguous. He made lame attempts to incriminate Ma Brewer's hidden friends. Bugs categorically denied the charges and stated that a collusion of nefarious villains was threatening his business. Objecting to this position, Ma's attorney grew more aggressive. In language drafted in the emotional style of the day, he challenged the defendant's testimony. It had no effect. The rigmarole came to a grinding halt when the trial ended and the jury shortly thereafter gave its verdict. Col. Hungerford's son, Bugs, was exonerated and held liable only for the cost of the piano.

After the trial ended feelings ran high; dozens of Ma Brewer's customers, led by Towhead, Dice, and Duck, gathered angrily outside the courthouse. Most of the customers were bitter because the drugs had been lost. Leaving the courthouse that afternoon was akin to running a gauntlet. The writer, Dukay Volney, seemed to be especially resentful about the loss of the laudanum. He was irate and accosted Fred W. Bergeron as he left the building. Attorney Bergeron responded by caning Volney as the writer cowered under his blows. Towhead, menacingly holding the butt of his pistol, then threatened Bergeron and Hungerford's son with their very lives. At that point, most good citizens dispersed for home and hearth with ominous forebodings. Ben found Bergeron's stogie in the bush beside the courthouse steps where the lawyer left it in his haste to evade the hostilities and gave it away to some man who was hoping to smoke the remains.

Next morning bright and early Hungerford's son was murdered while eating breakfast at the Washington Hotel. Bugs was well known in town, and most thought correctly that he had devoted himself wholly to hard drink and low company and thus was lost to the world. But however ungainly such behavior may be it did not justify his lamentable fate. While no proof yet existed with regard to who may have been the perpetrator, suspicions abounded. Sheriff J.H. Sanderson arrested Towhead at Ma Brewer's early the next morning. Sheriff Sanderson was able to retrieve Towhead from the bar without firing a shot only because he had surprised the desperados while they were counting their winnings at Ma's place from the night before. Even with the element of surprise, the situation had been tense and it helped to have a deputy accompany him with his double barrel scattergun loaded with buck shot. Sheriff Sanderson and his deputy slowly backed to the door with guns leveled and Towhead in cuffs. Dice, the sneering elegant, held his heavy pistol cocked and pointed down and Duck flashed his Bowie while fingering the derringer in his waistband. Both men threateningly followed the sheriff and his deputy to the door.

Thinking surely no more excitement would take place that day, Richard, Ben, and I snuck upstairs at Ma Brewer's and put an irritated opossum in Dukay Volney's room. Word was that the writer was out researching the mounds but we had seen him going into a side room unzipping his trousers and we knew he would be indisposed for a time. Then we retrieved our bateau and fished until after dark.

Our local citizens immediately became incensed after the killing. The men of the town demanded vengeance

for Bugs Hungerford and they got it. Having had a gut full
of these nefarious sharpers the men of our village decided
to hang the murderer. They had hopes the other scalawags
would leave after the lynching. After dark that very evening, about the same time we were coming in from fishing,
a lynch mob broke into the jail and wrestled Towhead into
a tumbrel and took him to the edge of town to expiate
his crimes upon the limb of an ancient oak. We docked
our boat and carrying the fish we caught we followed the
crowd to the edge of town.

Citizens gathered under the oak, their minds cloud-
ed by hatred and whiskey; they hurled scurrilous lampoons
at the prisoner. Stripped of his weapons and his hidden
derringer, Tow looked harmless. He was a middle-aged
man with a distended belly and a double chin. He was
hung by his neck until dead. Most present agreed that he
seemed neither to hear nor see; the savage noise and sights
of the crowd under the tree made no impression on him.
Perhaps the bitterness of death was already past; even his
advisories admitted the rascal was bold and impudent to
the very end. Ben, Richard, and I were stunned; we left the
hanging and the fish we had caught earlier that day and
returned to our homes to gather our thoughts.

Afterwards, nothing changed in our town. The
hanging of Towhead did not have the desired result. Ma
Brewer brought in another rascal from New Orleans; he
joined Dice and Duck and was even more threatening
than Towhead had ever been. Ma continued to thrive and
prosper and found another source for laudanum. Behind
the scenes, our male citizens continued to support Ma and
her brothel. Nothing changed at all except that Bugs and
Towhead were gone. Our little river town was exposed like
all river towns for what it was; it was diverse, prosperous,
and full of people breaking the law impudently. The boys
and I were stunned with what we discovered; by roaming
our village and seeing the hanging we thought that the evil
was only in our town. But by maneuvering our town we
continued growing up and learning about life. We received
an advanced education with regard to what life was like
and eventually we learned that every river town was like
ours and that all of us had potential for evil within.

Ma finally passed away and was given a lavish funeral

attended by the leaders of the community. With her business closed, the ruffians she had depended upon moved to Memphis and secured similar positions in the same field. After Ma's death, another madam named Blonde Victoria arrived with fallen girls and opened her business which Likewise thrived. And the river kept rolling.

The Mound Builders of Patilla

Just prior to dawn, my father and I pulled up at Dr. Hood's
home. It had started to storm and was cooling off rapidly;
for some reason it seemed the sun was reticent about
coming up this day. Dr. Hood walked out of his massive
stone house in the angle where Cherry and Halls Ferry
intersect. He closed the door softly behind him because his
wife and three children were still asleep. The screen on the
front door was ripped where the family dog had forced his
way in and out numerous times. Magnolia leaves crackled
under the doctor's shoes. He limped slightly because he
had sprained his ankle on stage during his performance
in the melodrama *Gold in the Hills* on the "Big Mama"
Sprague steamboat the night before. He proceeded down
the uneven sidewalk, pausing to stoop and pick up the
January 12, 1964 Sunday *Clarion Ledger*. He looked back
up at his bedroom window before he got into the car that
Dad had running and warm. "Mawning Jim!" he beamed.
"What a day to get that cannon up. I believe we will get
what we need off the Cairo before this day is done." We
nodded rather sleepily and pulled out of the circular drive
and headed toward the Sydney Home.

  We didn't talk as we rolled through town past the
Sisters of Mercy Convent, the Balfour house, and Anchuca
Mansion. We parked directly in front of the Sydney

building on Crawford Street. Rubbing his hands together to warm them, Doc went inside to make his rounds. Dad cut the motor off and followed in hopes of getting some coffee. I followed them in, opened the paper and settled in with a warm saucer of coffee and milk. I opened the newspaper; the headlines blared in bold print, "LAST CAIRO CANNON TO BE RAISED." I read until Doc finished about a half hour later. The three of us walked down the hall toward the front door. Doc, who was my Sunday school teacher, was telling me that this event today was a sufficient reason for missing church. Suddenly, an old lady in a wheelchair rolled up and blocked us at the door. She took an unlighted corn cob pipe out of her mouth and spoke. "Say, ain't you Doc Hood?" Dad tried to shoo her away but Doc said "let her speak, Jim." She continued. "My granny knew your grandfather, and even fed him after the Yankees took Vicksburg. I been knowing yo people for a long time and I knew yo mommy. Let me warn you Doc—be careful today, watch yo self now. This just may be your day!" She cackled with laughter and without another word rolled her chair down the hall toward the cafeteria. As she rolled away, one could hear her making an audible sucking sound on her dry pipe.

Doc muttered almost to himself, "My day? yes'um! I'll be careful."

On the way out of town we stopped for breakfast at the Seawall Café. A railroad man leaned on the counter nursing a hangover and growling at all the patrons. A soda route driver looked as if he had been out all night. He seemed uncomfortable in garb other than his route uniform, but he sauntered over to our table and commented on Doc's performance the night before. He still had a Dixie cup in his hand that smelled like bourbon. After greeting us, he pounded Doc's back and called out to the other patrons, "Here's the hero from *Gold in the Hills*." He staggered back to his stool tugging at his tie and mumbling "there's gold in them there hills."

W.T. Reynolds raised his large face from his plate in the back booth and loudly commented, "Doc you were very good last night but I prefer that gal who plays Nellie. She's a lot cuter than you are." Judging by the uproar of laughter, most of the diners present agreed.

General Hogan shuffled over on his ever-present walker
to shake Doc's hand and ask about the Cairo project while
a middle-aged waitress of questionable morals stepped
around the general to see what we were having to eat. She
called our order out to Pete at the grill.

    As I looked around the café, I noticed a man whom
I did not see walk in; it was almost as if he just appeared.
He sat at a back table; none of the waitresses noticed him.
No food was in front of him, no coffee. I felt a chill; I
shuddered. He was a tan, grizzled, mustachioed man and
he was dressed in a United States Navy sailor's uniform of
Civil War vintage. He appeared to be of medium height,
dark of complexion and haggard. I couldn't take my eyes
off him and he stared back silently. My mind raced. Was he
a barge worker, a naval vet, a re-enactor?

    While we ate, we watched a television mounted in
the corner. I'd been watching the newscaster for years.
An ice cream company located in Panther Burn had
taken sponsorship to a new level. The newscaster would
finish the ice cream commercial and take a bowl back
to the news desk with him. It never bothered me to see
him eating ice cream so early, but he was gaining weight
rapidly. This morning he spooned his ice cream while he
gave his report. "The date was December 12, 1862. The
USS Cairo was on patrol sixteen miles north of Vicksburg
when it struck the torpedo. It was the first war ship to ever
be sunken by torpedo. It only took the ironclad twelve
minutes to go under. After the first explosion occurred,
it was virtually all over. Nothing but the smokestacks
and the flag staff could be seen as the vessel sank under
the troubled waters to a depth of thirty six feet. It has
remained in place quietly since that day for 101 years, ten
months, six days, and one hour. The last cannon is to be
lifted today and further salvage is to occur this spring.
After this last cannon is lifted, the vessel, devoid of guns,
will be thirty tons lighter and that much easier to bring up."

    Out of the corner of my eye I could see the strange
figure watching with intense interest. Doc also watched the
report, but he was not really himself this morning. Oh he
was polite with all, but unlike his usual self he broke bread
in a quiet and pensive mood. After breakfast, I followed
Doc and my dad to the register to pay. Pete turned from

the smoking grill and opened the register drawer. He took Doc's money and looked directly at Doc while whispering, "Please Doc, be careful. We have a front coming in late this afternoon, snow mixed with freezing rain. You'll be out on the Yazoo. You know the Indians called the Yazoo the river of death, don't you?" He slammed the register as the waitress called another order, nodded at Dad and turned back to the grill.

We left the Seawall and headed to the car, unwrapping toothpicks as we walked. A Cadillac limo pulled in and parked across Washington Street from our car. Doc opened his car door and pointed out the River Commission driver. Dad put the car in gear and asked where the River Commission guy would be going this early in the morning. Doc replied, "To the Jackson airport to pick up the government man who is coming to view the Cairo project today." Doc slammed his door and we pulled out and rolled up North Washington toward the delta. Dad asked Doc whether that little woman in the wheel chair had upset him. Doc looked out his window as we motored past Anderson Tully Lumber Yard and sighed, "Jim, this day has been coming for a long time. It's more important than all my projects put together. The Sydney home, my medical clinic, the Kanawa. History is going to be made today and you know how I love history." Doc smiled and turned to me. "I just hate to be missing my Sunday school class today."

Dad asked, "Doc, is anything else bothering you?" Doc had no response and kept gazing out the window as we drove.

We continued on under the sad trees covered with moss into the lower delta just north of town. It was almost as if we were driving into a wet sponge. The sky was still dark but one could see the heavy clouds scudding past the moon. I was settling in for the ride when I was startled to see the man again. He was walking over the bridge on Alligator Bayou. I shuddered when we passed and the man waved at me and smiled. Neither my dad nor Doc noticed the man. I was dumbfounded, how could the man walk from the Seawall Café to Alligator Bayou quicker than we could drive?

After the drive up Highway 61, we turned down a

gravel road and parked in the woods near the Yazoo River. The ground was soft and mushy under our tires. There was very little wind; the moon was obscured now but the sky was lightening up over the east bank and the air was not heavy as of yet but it was bitterly cold for the Delta. We got out of the car and stood momentarily on the soft wet ground. We could hear the baying of hunting dogs. Doc exchanged glances with Dad and said, "Hear those hounds Jim? They are probably from Lost Tom Camp over on Steele Bayou." Doc retrieved his heavy jacket and his paddle out of the trunk and walked toward his faded green skiff. He tossed the wooden paddle onto the seat. The unnatural thump of the wood hitting the aluminum seat reverberated across the Yazoo into the grey trees on the other side. He began to get in the boat after walking through the sloppy buckshot mud. Dad and I followed. Doc sat in the bow muttering to himself, "It will be late this afternoon, maybe after dark, when we finish; what a big day for our community."

The salvage boats were anchored in the middle of the river; we couldn't help but stare at the massed concentration of mechanical might. Dad and I paddled out towards the dark hulking shadow of the flotilla. The murky water was like cold molasses. Long cranes angled in several directions hung over the barges and looped cable was silhouetted against the dawn sky. The name of the craft was barely visible in large printed letters on the bow, Star of the West-Port of New Orleans. But I was not looking at the boat; I saw the man I had noticed in the Seawall Café and on the bridge. He was high on the cable rigging over the barges, sitting happily as the sun began to rise. He appeared to be looking toward us but I couldn't tell. I looked at Dad and Doc and neither one had seen the man, just as they didn't notice him at the Seawall or back at Alligator Bayou.

The dark hulk began to come to life; lights came on. Unseen men began to stretch and yawn; divers and deck hands and others got up. The massive steel hull echoed when someone dropped a heavy piece of metal. In the distance, I could see another rowboat coming down river slowly.

We edged in next to the Star. A crewmember

reached over the deck's edge to help us on board. At about the same time, the other boat I had noticed nosed in silently next to us. One half inch of cold water had leaked into the craft. A large fisherman named McShane wrestled his bulk up the rusty ladder and shook hands with Doc and my father.

They headed toward the galley where we could hear voices and pots and pans clanging. Doc and the fisherman walked into the mess and over toward the steaming coffee pot. Doc greeted everybody cordially; he waved at the national park historian and walked toward a grizzled and overweight man standing over some charts. Captain W.A. Rigatoni of New Orleans extended his large paw to Doc. "Welcome aboard Doctor!" The television mounted on the wall was on. Capt. Rigatoni pointed up at the screen and said to Doc, who was sipping a cup of coffee, "that newsman will be here this morning with his crew."

Doc glanced up at the screen. The large bald newsman was doing another ice cream commercial and was actually digging into another bowl of Panther Burn Vanilla. Back at his news desk he stated in between spoonfuls, "now for your Mississippi and Louisiana headlines."

Doc muttered, "Two bowls already!"

Rigatoni walked back over to the coffee and began telling the divers about the government man who did not like the plans to raise the Cairo. The lead diver laughed, "Where was he when we found this baby?"

McShane walked up to the captain and the divers; he rubbed his red eyes. "You guys talking about the government? I can tell you this, when Uncle Sam gets a hard-on he gonna screw somebody." Laughing, McShane's massive hand thumped the lead diver on the back. Rigatoni and the divers looked at the man but did not smile.

Capt. Rigatoni snarled, "McShane, you been at the Finn & Feathers all night again?" Doc walked back to the coffee pot and eagerly drew another cup.

McShane growled, "Doc gimme a cup of dat coffee."

Doc smiled and said, "It isn't coffee. It's black paint with chicory."

McShane glared at the New Orleans workers now

coming in for breakfast. "Whatever. Gimme some!"

Captain Rigatoni introduced the new diver to the fisherman and Doc. "Mr. McShane is a commercial fisherman. He knows the river and is on board to help with the river and the location. Doctor Hood is…."

Cutting Rigatoni short, the diver blurted, "I know the Doc. He treated my mom one time and she's at the Sydney Home now."

A car horn honked loudly on the bank and Rigatoni looked out of the porthole. He sighed. "There's that drunken mayor again. Send a boat for him."

We could feel the engines and generators down below whirring, coughing, and vibrating on the metal deck under our feet. McShane and the barge cook, Kefus, were chatting. I heard Kefus tell McShane that he had worked on the river for a long time but this job worried him. "We're messing with a grave heah. T'aint smart; would you go dig up a grave and lift the body out? Same thing heah. Somebody gonna pay, I promise you!"

McShane laughed and said, "Kefus, how many of them guns have y'all lifted up off the boat under us? Is it twelve now? Next one is the back breaker, ain't it thirteen?"

Kefus whispered, "Mark my words McShane; you don't know what I know! We are more than fools to raise stuff off this boat; it's like taking clothes off a decayed corpse."

Another car horn blared. Captain Rigatoni cursed. "This ain't nothing but a taxi service dammit! Send a boat for that news crew and make sure that fat ass don't bring no ice cream on board."

Doc said to McShane, "Say! Isn't your boy with the Saints? They are on television this afternoon. I wish I could get home to see it."

McShane ignored the Doctor and turned to one of the divers, "Don't I know you from somewhere? Ain't you been raised down river on Blakely plantation?"

The diver replied, "Yeah. My father was the overseer."

"Didn't you go to Rolling Fork High School?" McShane questioned.

"Yeah" said the diver. "I was in class with your son

Johnny, played ball with him. Who does he play for now? I ain't seen him in years?"

Between bits of sausage and biscuit Brewer said, "He's a tight end with the Saints. They're on TV this afternoon."

All the crewmen out of New Orleans Fisher Projects had come to the mess and settled in at the table for breakfast. They had overheard the plantation comment and they glared at the diver and the fisherman. They began to pound the table. "What's for breakfast? We want Dobrage Cake from Gambino's!"

Chef Kefus slid a platter of sausage and eggs down the table and snarled at them, "No way. What you see is what you get."

One of the project boys said, "Shut yo pie hole old man!"

A thin light-skinned fellow with the crew clutched through his work shirt a discolored bone on a chain around his throat. He continued holding the bone through his work shirt and averted his eyes, refusing to look at anyone.

The national park historian had entered the mess and was engaged in a heated discussion with the mayor; the Fisher Project boys listened with interest. The mayor uttered some random point regarding the purpose of the USS Cairo and its trip up the Yazoo and the historian replied, "That's what the boat we are raising was doing in the Yazoo. I agree with you."

Captain Rigatoni walked past the two of them on his way to the chart desk. He turned and said to the scholarly looking historian, "My son is a history major at LSU. He told me that 90% of Lee's army that surrendered at Appomattox never owned a slave." The historian shook his head disdainfully.

Ignoring him, the Captain rapped the table, "All right, let's listen up! It's time to get to work."

The two divers, the national park historian and the doc approached the table. The mayor stood sullen in a rumpled suit as the news crew began to set up cameras and lights while the anchorman had his baldhead and cheeks powdered to reduce the intense gleam for the benefit of his viewers. Rigatoni spoke. "Our job today is twofold.

First, lift the last cannon, the thirteenth, off the vessel below us. This cannon is the big mama; it is a 42-pounder army rifle cannon. Its weight is 8,465 pounds. We have already lifted twelve cannons off the boat and if you remember several of them were an all-day deal because of the river current and the weight of the guns. This gun is the heaviest one yet. Maybe our historian will tell us something about its size."

The historian hastily finished a mouthful of breakfast, adjusted his spectacles, and stammered, "It is an 1841 model with a bore diameter of seven inches and a barrel length of 110 inches and an overall length of over ten feet. Once it is up, the vessel will be thirty tons lighter when you count all the other cannons. I helped locate the Cairo with two other men in 1956. After many years of frustrations and setbacks, we are on the verge of being amply rewarded for our efforts. This is the most important single day in recovery efforts since we became convinced that the ship was still intact. It is the thrill of a lifetime. Early in the Civil War seven of these ships were docked along the river at Cairo, Illinois. They must have been striking to observe, the Cairo, the Carondelet, the Cincinnati, the Mound City, the Baron De Kalb, the Louisville and the Pittsburgh. This ship beneath us is the last one surviving and bringing it up will honor the vessels and crews on both sides that fought for the river that controlled America's future."

Looking up from the charts and thanking the historian, Capt. Rigatoni continued. "Ok Doc, while you are up give us an update on the skeleton we found last week." Doc replied, "Well I know it was human, no doubt about that. The question is who and what. The Doc cleared his throat, adjusted his glasses, and continued. "The diver found the skeleton last Sunday near number three gun port and brought it to the surface immediately. I examined the bones; some damage had been done to parts of the skeleton, whether by external blows or violence we have no way of knowing. The commander of the Cairo, Capt. Selfridge, reported no loss of life or serious injuries during the sinking. Therefore the bones are a mystery of significance. We have shipped the skeleton intact to the Smithsonian Institution so the curator of physical anthropology can make a decision with regard to whom and what we have found. I have my own opinion; it was not Union naval personnel or a confederate prisoner. My personal thoughts are that it could have been brought aboard by one of the sailors on the boat sunken below us. The Cairo was on many occasions near the various mound builder sites which abound in this area. In fact, there are several less than a mile from this spot at Blakely plantation. Perhaps it was as simple as a grave robber trying to impress his friends."

At that point, I noticed the mysterious man again. I rose in my chair; I knew something was amiss. I watched, worried and fearful. The mysterious sailor was staring at the worker with the bone around his neck. The Captain continued. "What are river diving conditions today?" The diver replied, "Capt. Rigatoni, both of us have done salvage work from the Persian Gulf to the Great Lakes, but this river is the most unpredictable I've ever seen."

Rigatoni laughed. "Well nothing can be done about that. How about diving conditions?"

The diver studied his chart and said, "Weather conditions are favorable until just before dark; then all hell breaks loose. But diving conditions are different. I miss diving in clear water; this Yazoo is worse than the mud on the shore of Lake Maurepaux. You can't see anything. But we'll have that cannon up by dark."

Capt. Rigatoni looked at the mayor. "What time is the government man getting here?"

With a singsong lilt the mayor came to life. "Oh this morning sometime. He's flying into Jackson and being limoed out here. I guarantee he'll be here for lunch." Everybody in the mess chuckled.

Rigatoni finished. "Now what we are gonna do after we get this gun up is take a test strain so we can begin the process of working this boat out of its hole and moving it onto the sunken barge we will put in place next week. By then we will have twenty-two cables under the Cairo's hull and tied to barges on either side so the battleship will be in an underwater sling. Now, this is where it hits the fan and when our divers will be most important to our salvage. But that is next week. We have enough to do today. Let's go get that last cannon."

Chairs scraped and dinnerware clanked as the

workers got up to report to duty. Within minutes motors were running and roaring; smoke drifted across the river into the cypress forest on the other side. I had not noticed the mysterious man leaving and he was nowhere in sight. Rigatoni and Doc went to the command center in the pilothouse. I followed them. Dad stayed in the mess engaged in conversation with our mayor. In the pilothouse, Rigatoni nodded and a crewman pulled a lever, which gunned a motor and the salvage barge slowly engaged. I was watching when the captain turned to Doc and said, "This is the last one Doc, and after this cannon we go after the gal herself!"

I saw the huge crane swing to a stop over the spot, which McShane had indicated with an upside down milk jug anchored to a car part he had found in his yard. The cable and crane creaked and whirred; drifting logs bumped the side of the Star of the West as it struggled to position itself over the Cairo. The boat lurched and cold water splashed up on several of the deck crew who were trying to anchor the Star over the Cairo's grave. Rigatoni was really focused because when the exact spot over the vessel was reached he would have to shut down the motor. Within minutes we reached the spot and the captain ordered all engines shut down and anchors in place. In the ensuing silence, we could hear the steeple bells at Trinity Church in Vicksburg fifteen miles away. Doc told the captain, "Listen—you can hear the church bells clear as day; that's a good omen. Sound carries in winter doesn't it? No doubt we'll get this boat up soon."

After that comment I went back below decks to gather my thoughts. I was sitting in the engine room alone when the mysterious sailorman entered through the bulkhead and approached me. I looked desperately for a way to flee. But there was no way out. He walked over near me and stood and stared. The uniform he was wearing looked very old and his shoes were like nothing I had ever seen. I was confused and frightened, but oddly that feeling of fear began to vacillate and vacate my senses. The sense of confusion remained but I felt much calmer; I was not threatened. In fact, I ascertained that the man wanted to communicate with me somehow without speaking. No words or sound emanated from his mouth but somehow his thoughts were transmitted most clearly. I understood him to indicate that I was an old soul in a young body; that I would be able to see what others did not. He wanted me to hear his story, because he was here for reasons I may not fathom.

He was from New Madrid, Missouri; he had been a sailor in the Federal navy on the USS Cairo. His grandfather and grandmother had lost their lives in the New Madrid earthquake of 1811. His mom ran a boarding house and his father was a rapscallion. His brother was killed at Gettysburg while fighting for the Confederacy. When the Cairo cruised up the Yazoo during the Vicksburg siege, the ironclad anchored near Blakely plantation and he robbed a grave in a burial mound. He removed the skeleton from its final resting place in the mound. He and his crewmates on the USS Cairo hung it near gun port number three and officers and sailors alike made fun of it. He indicated that he regretted that action and he had come from a parallel plane to make amends. He had returned only because he was allowed to do so by the Supreme Being. He was back on earth correcting his mistake and repenting of his sin so he could move on to another level of spirit. His reason for coming was not to terrify or wreak violence; he was merely here to rectify his past mistake and to make adjustment in the eyes of the Master. He was in fact choosing life not death, and he was here to harm no one. However, there would be a death in the river this evening, but it had nothing to do with him; it was simply the man's time. Before I had any time to think about what he was communicating he finished with a thought that people have always been the same no matter what the era; no matter whether they were salvage employees or important politicians. They are just reflections of the way this material plane is and will be.

I remained in the room for several hours, processing what the sailor had told me. As the afternoon waned, I found myself looking out the porthole. I saw the diver surface on the starboard side of the Star. He gave a thumb up to signal that he had hooked the thirteenth cannon. I went up on deck; the newsman was already posed with the diver in view to his rear. Cameras rolling, he began to let the public know what a magnificent historical moment was taking place. One of his camera crew called, "We got that shot Bob!"

About that time, the limo pulled up on the bank with the Washington bureaucrat inside. He retrieved his briefcase from the chauffer and stood on the bank tapping his foot as he waited for a boat to come get him. Capt. Rigatoni cursed and sent a boat to get the man. In their need to return to the station and edit their work, the TV crew hurried to pack and clambered aboard the departing craft for a ride to the shore.

We all gathered on the deck in a slight snow flurry under heavy skies to examine the old gun. Doc was ecstatic with delight and posed for pictures with the historian, the captain, the divers, and the government man. We stood off to the starboard side near the weapon and stared at it, waiting, wondering.

After a few minutes, McShane said, "Well Kefus, the thirteenth cannon is up and nothing happened."

Kefus whispered, "I ain't worried about the cannon fool. One of them project boys took a small piece of that skeleton, the right patella I think. He thought nobody would miss it. He drilled a hole in it and made a necklace. That's what I'm worried about." He pointed to the lanky young man on the deck. "He's wearing it now. You don't mess with skeletons. Somebody'll pay!" McShane stared blankly at the necklace, as if unable to process the information.

Doc complemented Capt. Rigatoni and the men on a job well done. He offered congratulations all around and explained that he hoped to catch his family at church. The sheriff's deputy on the bank had agreed to take him back to town. The doctor began to pack his stuff in his row boat. Then he got in his boat and rowed off toward the bank. Dad and I waved goodbye.

Capt. Rigatoni and the divers broke open a bottle of whiskey. Everybody started toward the mess; I was walking just behind the young man with the bone necklace. Sounds of the televised football game came through the open hatch. A poker game had started up in the corner; one of the New Orleans boys dealing the cards was telling a joke and he finished with "dat stripper used the Tulane guy's pecker to stir her drink." Everybody in the mess roared with laughter.

I was not surprised to see the Cairo sailor enter through the wall and approach the young man with the bone necklace. The ancient sailor did not hesitate. He walked up to the man and jerked the necklace off. Then he left immediately after winking at me. The man was visibly upset; he thought someone in the room had done it. He ran around the room like a chicken with its head removed. He was furious. Nobody could calm him down.

I went back out on deck; it was cold and slippery. I could see the historian shuffling nervously near the uplifted cannon watching Doc paddle toward the bank. As it turned dark, I stood off to the side and closed my eyes and whispered a prayer of travel mercies for Dr. Hood. Several moments later, I heard a weak cry through the gathering gloom. "I'm in the water! Help me!"

We could hear Doc continuing to call. Dad ran inside the mess and yelled "Captain! Turn your klieg lanterns on. Doc fell in the river; we can't see him." Lights squelched on and all I saw was the little green boat slowly drifting in circles in the cold muddy water.

With others from the Star, Dad, the captain, and I reached the riverbank within minutes. Rigatoni had radioed for help and several county deputies soon joined us on the river bank. The captain warned the law officers that the river was very dangerous. The weather was changing. The river had become so swift that an accumulation of drift was causing the project lifting barges to strain from their moorings. The river had risen four feet since the morning, and the rise was creating an unusually swift current that was bringing large amounts of drift down river. This drift was pounding against the barges, which were located crossways in the stream above the sunken boat. The pressure was increasing on the mooring and lifting cables and they were in danger of tearing loose from their holdings. All in all a bad report. After listening, the deputies backed down the bank and launched two boats to search for Dr. Hood.

A variety of vehicles began to arrive and park in the mud with lights on and motors running. The bank had a thin ice sheen upon it and was very slippery. Various officials and law enforcement folks called from their warm homes maneuvered on the bank, shining lights, walking, looking. The local funeral director slushed to a halt in his caddy, emerged from the car and walked toward the river, getting buckshot mud on his Florsheims. He hollered at the two bulky deputies in the boats with grappling hooks. One of the deputies on shore whispered to another, "Where is the Sheriff? Running his gals on Mulberry? We need him out here. Who's going to tell Doc's wife?"

The other deputy walked toward his squad car. "Don't worry. I'll radio the sheriff again!"

The funeral director's breath was visible in the night as he joked with a local constable. The funeral man said, "When I got the call I was at Goldie's and I had spilt so much BBQ on my tie that they tried to charge me for a takeout order." He looked out over the moving water and mused to the officer next to him, "Well, he'll likely be hung up on Desoto Island by tomorrow." Then the funeral director wrapped his topcoat closer around his body and started back toward his black caddy; a random mamma hound sniffed his pants cuff. He kicked her away. Once in the car he lowered the driver's window and called to his assistant, "Leave the hearse out here just in case. I will make it back into town in time for Sunday night services at Crawford Street. His wife and kids should be there."

A group of officers began to question Dad and me. "No one really saw it," Dad said.

"Did he slip?" an officer asked.

"No, he never made the bank," Dad replied.

"Did he call out?" asked another.

Dad responded tiredly, "Yes, he called out 'I'm in the river.' That was it."

"Where did he fall in?" asked the first deputy. Dad nodded towards the river. The deputy turned and looked with unease at the swirling Yazoo.

I don't know where it came from, but I told him, "Don't fret officer; you won't find his body."

I could see the cops standing on the river bank shivering. They shined their lights into a little indent in the bank. "Looks like he may have slipped in right here. Yeah I see where he caught the grass."

The other officer said, "He didn't slip in. He was in the Yazoo when he went down."

I shook my head and leaned on the still warm hood

of the deputy's squad car. I looked out at the Star of the West; lights glaring on the water made it look as if it were ice and one could walk out to the boat. I looked away sadly and I saw the mysterious sailor walking across river as if it were solid land. He reached the bank and just faded into the woods. The icy water soaked into my shoes. The whole matter was stunning. I felt empty but some measure of illumination that I did not understand had occurred. Dr. Hood was gone. I stood on the Yazoo River bank in perplexity regarding the great mystery of life and death that had been shown to me.

No trace of Doc was ever found. Smithsonian tests on the skeleton proved it to be what appeared to be the remains of an ancient mound builder that had lived in the area centuries before the Civil War. Speculation held that the skeleton had been removed by federal naval personnel on board the USS Cairo from the nearby mounds on Blakely Plantation. The Smithsonian added a codicil to the report given; the skeleton was going to be exhibited in the Smithsonian museum, but the skeleton was now missing. An attendant claimed that a person in an old navy uniform with proper papers had retrieved the bones late one night and took them away.

Chief Verisimilitude

They called him Chief. He played college football at Vanderbilt and had played professional football for several teams. Chief was a full-blooded Indian of the Chickasaw tribe; he was born in Tennessee and had returned there after the close of his career. Two of his former teammates in college and one from the pro ranks decided to hold a gathering in Memphis in honor of Chief for his impending birthday one January. Bobby Weller, Chief's quarterback in the pro ranks, and two of his teammates in college, Jerry Andrews and Alton Teller, planned to meet at the Peabody Hotel and celebrate with Chief.

The first to arrive was Bobby. He drove up from the Mississippi Delta town of Panther Burn. Weller matriculated down Union Avenue in his Fleetwood Caddy. The city shined in the winter rain. Nearing the Peabody Hotel, Bobby slowed and tipped his Stetson to the statue of Nathan Bedford Forrest, which stood near the avenue. He continued down Union, pulled into the hotel drive and parked at the curb in front of the Peabody. The tall rangy man exited the car. He tossed his cigarette to the sidewalk and stretched his frame. His body was that of an ex-athlete, still muscular and powerful. The doorman approached the caddy and kiddingly asked Weller whether the oil embargo was causing him any inconvenience.

Bobby laughed, tossed him the keys and shook his head
in the negative while mentioning that he had to stay in
line for two hours down in Rolling Fork to get his gas. He
handed a ten spot to the doorman, turned, and started
toward the lobby.

Chief and another man cycled into the drive
before Bobby entered the lobby. Chief got off his bike
and removed his helmet and goggles. Weller turned and
instantly recognized the face he had known when they
played together. Chief's body still bore the requirements
of his former trade. Muscular and powerful, he was a
handsome man of striking appearance. His face was of
slender symmetry with a firm chin. His eyes were full and
liquid; their shadows varied from pure hazel to intense
and brilliant jet. Above his copper skin was a profusion
of straight black hair from which a forehead of unusual
breadth gleamed forth. Weller called to Chief, "Birthday
boy it is time to party. You look like you could play this
Sunday."

Chief replied, "I'd love to Bobby. But my best
friend, Bruiser, just died and I probably couldn't handle it
anyway."

Bobby reached out to shake hands. "You ain't
changed a bit Chief, and you look just like you did under
that helmet. Where you been?"

"We left Texas after Bruiser's funeral and came
through Arkansas hoping to get to the birthday party in
time. Mostly it was a smooth trip until just now when we
crossed the river. The wind was nasty as we weaved in
and out of traffic and emerged from a haze and fog as we
approached Chickasaw Bluffs."

Bobby laughed, "You mean Memphis don't you?"

"Yes," replied Chief, "if you insist. You're the
quarterback."

"Chief, what happened to Bruiser?"

Chief reached into his saddlebag to retrieve his ditty
bag. "He was thrown off his motorcycle after he failed to
negotiate a curve and crashed into some rocks 45 miles
south of nowhere. Bruiser was his own man, eccentric on
and off the field, but he was too young to die."

Bobby clapped Chief on the shoulder. "Well enough
of that. Happy birthday! Let's get checked in and have

a drink." Bobby and Chief walked toward the lobby.
They entered the Peabody, got registered, and took the
elevator up to the room. The man who rode in with Chief
remained quietly beside his motorcycle.

A dirty cab pulled up to the hotel. The Ann Peebles'
song "I Can't Stand the Rain" vibrated from the speakers
over the portico. Two large bulky guys emerged from
the cab. They had been linemen and blocked for Chief
when he was a running back at Vanderbilt. They had
flown in from Atlanta after changing flights. Jerry Rogers
was a college professor up East and Alton Teller was an
Episcopal priest in Nashville. Both were articulate and
well-educated. They got out of the cab discussing air
travel. The Rev. Teller was speaking. "Maybe the worst
was last month's Andes crash. Sixteen of forty-five of that
rugby team survived only because they broke a cultural
taboo of a foundational nature."

"Yes, I read about that horrible situation and how
they made it through, but I can't fault them," Professor
Rogers responded. "Do you know the work of Robert
Smithson, a young star of the New York City art world?
He was hired to consult on the new Dallas-Fort Worth
Airport. He said in his writings that air travel had power to
work on the inner life of many and it could be an object
of fascination, fear ... whatever. Maybe that would explain
the Andes deal."

Alton lifted his bag out of the trunk. "Oh yeah,
I remember Smithson. His premise was that flying was
not material but was equally a mental construct. It was
not simply a mode of transportation but an idea, a fragile
dream. But, you're stretching a bit to link it to the Andes
cannibalism." Jerry slammed the cab trunk and he and
Alton walked past the thin man slouching beside his bike.

The man who had arrived with Chief was well
knit and compact. He appeared to be neither robust nor
remarkable, but a menacing expression emanated from
his face. He had a large villainous mouth; his wrinkled
forehead bore upon it the stamp of myriad years. His grey
hair was a record of the past and his eyes seemed sibyls
of the future. In appearance, the man seemed an ancient
icon of darkness. His bike tag read PHAROAH. He had
raven feathers on his gas tank and in his beard. He came

across as most threatening. Both Alton and Jerry sensed the menace. They averted their eyes and continued past looking at a newspaper dispenser for the *Commercial Appeal*, which featured headlines regarding President Nixon and his growing troubles, before proceeding to the hotel desk to register.

Bobby and Chief settled into their room. Bobby poured two shots of Black Jack and they imbibed while they looked out at the bridge to Arkansas. They noticed that another storm was blowing in from across the river. Chief walked over and turned the television on. He asked Bobby if he had noticed the people gathered around the lobby television. "Naw, I was signing autographs for my fans."

Chief searched channels trying to locate the breaking news story. "Well, you missed a big story Bobby. There was a shootout at the Howard Johnson hotel in New Orleans and many are likely dead."

Ignoring Chief, Bobby began talking about the championship game in which he and Chief had played. "Remember the 1958 championship game? Yankee Stadium was full. It was sudden death overtime. What a game!"

Frowning, Chief muttered, "All I remember was overtime when the Colts were on our 8 yard line and that guy from the network ran out on the field and created a distraction."

Bobby smiled. "Oh you know the Network had him go out to give them time to re-hook some wires."

"And I remember that I was traded that next year," Chief continued. "And my rookie card picture looked like a Lakota Sioux brave with a bad haircut." Chief found the breaking news channel and listened as the commentator updated the violent and tragic situation.

Bobby poured more Black Jack. "Well, don't feel bad. They started Heinrich instead of me. I remember our drive in the 4th quarter with my 46-yard completion to Schnelker and then Gifford took it in on the next play. If Coach Barrett had not made us punt with 4th and inches and less than 2 minutes left we would have beat those SOBs." Bobby drained his shot. "Then in overtime Maynard fumbled and threw us off. Our defense was tired;

they drove 80 yards and Ameche scored and it was over."

"Yes, Bobby it is over," grumbled Chief as he turned from the television.

"Today, everybody gets big rings for games like that," Bobby lamented.

Chief put his glass down. "All I got was being traded, but you got that Marlboro man contract and those shoe stores and big money. Me? I got a ripped knee and a lifelong headache."

The newsman excitedly spoke into his handheld microphone. "We are live at the Howard Johnson's in New Orleans. We now have numbers: two firemen wounded and one policeman dead. No speculation on who the shooter is or what he wants."

Bobby turned to Chief. "Who is that man traveling with you?"

"Oh just a fellow I met at Bruiser's wake. The only thing he ever spoke about was some Delta crossroads at midnight. I've never seen him eat anything since we've been traveling together."

Bobby pulled a Smith & Wesson out of his waistband and said, "Well, I got a bad feeling about that guy. Don't let that pecker near me tonight birthday boy! By the way, how was Bruiser's funeral? He had a rough go at life. We drafted him in the 2nd round but he was with the Giants only 25 days. Coach Barrett traded him when he refused to get his ankles taped. Then he refused to run a play in for his new team, the Colts. He told Eubanks to get another messenger boy. He deliberately ran the wrong way in practice to make things more challenging for himself. Then, on his third team he slugged a coach on the Redskins, was cut, went to Nam, came back and played for the Saints. But he hadn't changed. He skipped practice saying perfection was impossible so why practice. He only ran the ball three times that year in New Orleans for 3 yards. He was not coachable. A nut case."

"Bobby, you don't understand. He became a very spiritual person."

Laughing, Bobby said, "I don't give a damn what he is or was. Let's go see if the bar is open."

The former Vanderbilt offensive linemen finished checking in and took the elevator up to their room. They tossed their suitcases on the beds. Alton had noticed the lobby television broadcasting breaking news about the shootout in New Orleans and he immediately turned on the tube hoping to catch the latest. He stopped switching channels as soon as he heard the frantic newscaster's tremulous voice. After the update, the station shifted back to *The Edge of Night*. Alton shut the tube off, shaking his head sadly at the senseless carnage. As they unpacked, Jerry asked, "Did you see the explosion of the housing project when we were flying in and landing?"

"I did, how could anyone on board the airplane miss it?" Alton replied.

"I read last week that some pundits considered the demolition to represent a symbolic death of modernism. How can you explain the blowing up of the most advanced housing project in our nation? I think that the Great Society of Lyndon is being improperly challenged."

"Explanations for the failure of the housing project are extremely complex," Alton replied. "Some have cited architectural factors, some cite economic decline, others mention white flight or lack of employed tenants. The Great Society of Lyndon was doomed from the beginning. Progressives attempted to turn our cities into labs of social reform but crime and decay have set in. Face it Jerry, the social justice agenda where every pot has a chicken in it and every driveway has a new Impala will continue to fail."

Jerry got up. "I don't think so. But whatever. Let's go find Chief and party."

When Jerry and Alton arrived downstairs, the gathering for Chief's party was complete. Everyone stood around the piano and sang "Happy Birthday" to their friend. After the singing, they left the piano and took places at a table and began to catch up with each other, chatting and talking and drinking. Chief apologized for his attitude; he said it was a result of his friend's death and would be temporary. But his desolate countenance belied his words. Jerry and Alton were delighted to see their old teammate and they immediately began discussing the highpoint of their college football career together, the Gator Bowl. Alton said, "Chief, I'll never forget how you carried all three of those Auburn guys into the end zone. You were unstoppable. You must have gained over a 100 yards in that game. After the Gator Bowl that year, everyone called you Chief Verisimilitude."

"Why?" asked Chief. "I always wondered about that nickname."

Alton laughed. "It was a term of endearment. Remember those helmets we wore then with that big V on both sides? That's why the team nicknamed you."

Chief was glad to see them and polite but he was not really into the conversation. He smiled vaguely and said, "I never knew that. I thought it was critical."

Alton and Jerry could tell that Chief was somewhat preoccupied, but a rapid smile shot over Chief's face in response to their questions about his being picked in the first round by the Giants and how he kept his college number 24 when he went pro. The discussion continued about football until the professor turned it into an intellectual diatribe about the meaning of the sport. Jerry said that he had been lecturing on the topic to his students. He said that our society's former ruggedness was most apparent now in sports. Bobby listened intently as Andrews stated that our American frontier had disappeared and that we now lived in a state of moral decay associated with its loss. He cited as an example the shootout in New Orleans which was currently occurring. Bobby was so disgusted that he placed his Smith & Wesson on the table to accentuate the point that frontier still lived. Jerry immediately moved to another seat and began talking with Alton. Bobby then joined Chief who was drinking alone at the bar and discussed life with the New York Giants.

Jerry nodded toward the bar and said to Alton, "That guy reminds me of an article that said in our society stardom was a virus infecting everything. I agree with whoever said that we are not a global village—we are a global outpatient clinic."

Sipping his water, Alton said, "Our society is marked by neurotic undercurrents and contains a collection of symptoms which could be included on a hospital chart." Another Ho Jo update came on as they talked and watched the news on TV. The death toll had risen. A honeymooning couple had been found murdered in their room and a fireman had just been shot and fallen off the ladder to his death. Police officers had made it to the roof and blasted away at a stairwell cover where the killer was suspected to be hiding. "Look at this gunfight. It is almost as if killers are celebrities now," Alton said to no one particular. "So many of us have a nascent desire for celebrity that is replacing our desire for money or power. Young people have exchanged collective transformation for personal transformation. During the past ten years a new radical individualism has dawned. I am not surprised that last year birth rates in our country reached the lowest in our history. We are a different country than we were a decade ago; we face moral crisis and the impending collapse of our established institutions."

"But listen Alton," Jerry interjected, "this repressive system must be brought down, and the one who does it should be a celebrity."

"Jerry, you're missing a point most important and I hope you aren't teaching your students such bunk. The debunking or failure of one system inevitably paves the way for another. It is paradoxical that the intense need to cast off one form of authority is accompanied by an equally intense search for a replacement. We've cast off God and now we seek other gods." Bobby and Chief had returned to the table and they looked bored and unhappy; neither was listening.

"You are wrong Alton," Jerry said. "Look at our celebs today, Charles Manson, Rev. Moon, and Russell Means. All have contributed in their own manner. It's true that we are being jolted by a series of shocks and institutional failures in our society, and maybe the shift will evoke expressions of systemic, perhaps irreparable, crisis, but that's a good thing."

The bartender turned the television up as the newsman excitedly told the listeners that the Howard Johnson shooter had been eliminated and the crisis was over. Bobby stood, clapped, cheered, and waved his pistol. Alton sighed, "This oedipal crisis will leave us still with a need for a father. The crisis will not abate; it will intensify."

"Bartender! Another round please," Jerry called. Bobby's chair scraped as he got up to leave. "Boys this conversation done gave me a headache."

That night Madam Gardenia sent a limo to the

Peabody for the group. The celebrants had showered and changed and were ready to dine. "Where we going to eat?" asked Bobby.

"At Hazeltine's, an old brothel," the driver replied. "Madam Gardenia bought the building and operates her restaurant there now. It's just a short drive from the Peabody." A few minutes later they pulled up outside a two-story brick building built just before the Civil War. The birthday party was ushered through the crowded public dining area to a private dining room with elegant furnishings and a bar decorated in Chief's honor with the colors of three teams for which he played: Vanderbilt, New York and Minnesota. A trio composed of clarinet, guitar, and drums played softly in the corner. Chief took the head of the table, but he was even more distracted and quiet than he had been that afternoon. His mood was casting a shadow over the proceedings.

The waiters hovered, taking orders for drinks and appetizers. The professor jokingly used a term that a literary critic had coined in visceral disgust with regard to Erica Jong's recent novel—he tried to order a rare pudenda. Bobby stared in disbelief. No one laughed with the exception of Alton, and the professor was informed by the waiter that pudenda was not on the menu. Conversation continued while the waiters began to bring sumptuous meals to serve the men. As the party progressed, Jerry and Alton noticed a program on the television elevated in the corner. It was the premier episode of *The Loud Family Documentary* with eleven episodes to follow. Both had read about the upcoming documentary and were aware that the opening show highlighted basics on the family, their lovely home in California's coastal mountains, a swimming pool, four cars, a recording studio, and five kids. They watched the show as they ate.

After dinner Madam Gardenia emerged from the kitchen with a cake for Chief. With her full bodied frame, she swooped around the table. She appeared happy, dauntless and sagacious. Her spirit was vibrant, and her presence exuded a profuse out flowing of wisdom. Madam cut and served the cake to all. While the dessert was served, Bobby went to the restroom. As he returned,

he was accosted by several autograph seekers. He proudly
sauntered into the private dining room with them, saying,
"Follow me wasted fans and cows of Basham. There
is cake enough for all." Most who accompanied Bobby
into the private room partook of the cake, paid birthday
respects to Chief and departed slightly embarrassed.

The dining room gradually emptied and those
remaining sat around the table to talk. The party now
included a doctor, one of Bobby's fans and his wife, and
a circuit judge from Mississippi. Coffee was served and
the discussion continued in earnest as the television was
turned off. The doctor commented on the first *Loud Family*
episode. He thought they were a wonderful beautiful
family. "I look forward to watching the other episodes.
Our nation can be proud of them."

Jerry disagreed. "Doctor, how can you praise the
opulent and elite when so many are hungry?"

On the other hand, Alton had sensed that
beneath the outward appearance of enviable privilege
and happiness laid a different reality of long simmering
tensions. Alton posited, "Doctor, this is a new reality of
the family and at the same time a media invasion of our
lives. You best watch the whole series before you heap
praise on them. "

Chief still sat at the head of the table. He was
filled with an inconceivable agitation. Everyone present
breathed the atmosphere of sorrow. An air of stern, deep,
and irredeemable gloom hung over the dining room.
The birthday gathering had entered a region infinitely
drearier than any yet seen. In fact, a close observer could
have seen a tear or two rolling down Chief's face. In low
volume difficult to hear and with words tremulous and few,
Chief mentioned an Indian prophecy. With a hurried and
gibbering murmur he stated, "My people have a prophecy
that is very important. It says that we live beside a living
river which flows deep, wide, and swift. Our job is to enter
the living water and let God take us to our destination.
But most of us won't enter because of fear and ego. We
cling desperately to the shore. The result is that simmering
questions have boiled over, thorny ones kept at bay for
centuries on the back burners. Why is the world like it is?
Why do we suffer so? Why is my best friend buried and

rotting beneath the Texas sand? I will walk to the Father of Waters after this party."

The celebrants shifted uncomfortably. Bobby got up and walked over to the musical trio. They were packing up, but he offered them $20 for three more songs. They accepted and Bobby sauntered back to the table and asked the fan's wife to dance with him. She accepted and they spun away to the music. Alton addressed Chief with concern. "Chief, the problem is that your cosmology has been ripped away."

Chief muttered, "It's been a long dry season. My soul is curled up within. I am raging and struggling. How could things have gone like they have?"

Alton thought before he offered some solace to Chief. "Such rage would not exist unless you thought a real God existed behind the fraudulent one. So your belief is a quivering spark that can be again fanned into a flame. Obviously you know there is a God. You have an expectation of God. Maybe it's the common illusion many of us have that God fails us. But what is really happening is that the lesser God in our illusion exposes the fraudulent God and reminds us of what Meister Eckhart expounded upon: 'God save me from God.' The point is only that our illusions fail and, whatever else happens, the real and true God is there for us."

Bobby and the fan's wife swirled past the table. The woman's husband threw his napkin on the table in disgust and exited with a scowl on his face. The doctor passed a bottle of pills across the table to Chief and said, "Here, this will fix it all." Chief angrily slapped the pills out of his hand and cursed.

Jerry shook his head. "Don't talk that way Chief. The doctor is a good man. He takes care of Elvis. Maybe medicine is all you need to get over whatever is bothering you. This is the modern world; everyone takes something."

Madam Gardenia took a seat at the table and Likewise Bobby and the fan's wife finished their dance and sat down still holding hands. Sitting next to Chief, Alton whispered, "Yes Chief, we suffer, but don't hold back your questions. Don't cave into despair. Many of us transgress through a fury of rage and unbelief, but the continuation of our journey signals a deeper faith. Compare Psalm

23 with its green pastures and still waters with Psalm 88. The majority of us love 23 because 88 shows real spiritual agony and crushing bleakness is offered. Not even a faint whisper of hope is offered. But we must realize that despite the raging despair, Psalm 88 is a poem of deep faith because the valley of the shadow of death is not just a possibility but the actual spot from which the writer prays. So remember our primal indestructible diamond of faith is formed under the unfathomable pressures of feeling utterly abandoned and betrayed by God. You'll be fine my brother. Hang in there."

A waitress rushed into the dining room. "Madam I need you over here! Somebody got in the front door before we locked it." The icon of evil pushed the waitress aside and stepped in the door.

Madam got up. "What do you want Jupiter?" The man stood silently and stared. Madam addressed the man. "You are not welcome here, please leave now!" He turned and sauntered toward the door, uttering something unintelligible. Madam sat back down and lit a large cigar.

Jerry said, "Madam we saw him this afternoon at the Peabody, do you know him?"

Madam sighed. "His name is Jupiter Johnson. I knew him downriver in the Delta. He is way off the track. He calls himself the Raven."

The judge spoke up. "Madam, I know him also; he appeared in my court in Vicksburg numerous times for various offences. I haven't seen him in years. I heard he was out West. There was a story around town about him going to the crossroads and selling his soul, but I didn't buy it."

"Judge," Madam said, "the man is dangerous and evil. He is the epitome of darkness. I saw him lurking in the alley out back about an hour or so ago and recognized him. I asked him then to vacate the premises and he just stared."

Chief offered quietly, "He's a friend of mine. He's looking for me."

Madam blew a cloud of cigar smoke toward the ceiling, collected her thoughts and said quietly to Chief, "I don't mean to butt in, but I have overheard the conversations. I never have even seen a football game. We don't really know each other but may I say something? Jupiter or Raven, whatever you call him, will not lead you where you want to go. Only God will do that. In Greek theatre there is something called Peripeteia. The term means reversal or a turning point. In tragic drama it is the shift of one's fortune from good to bad. Such a view is essential to the plot of a tragedy, but we can understand it in a different way. Going through Peripeteia and facing its agony brings a complete reversal in a person's understanding of his or her life. When we face such a moment we breakdown and are plunged into the deepest kind of pain imaginable. In the throes of it, we can only rage, weep or blow our self away. Many of us believe that we are masters in life, but the truth is that the illusion we hold brings our fall. Life conspires to bring us to the point of realization that contrary to everything we had known or hoped we actually have no control, no mastery. Of course, we refuse to accept our smallness. We hold on to our illusions. But we are not masters of our destiny. We are small, frail, contingent creatures. Our lives run like water to the lowest point. But this tragic moment is in reality a blessing. It is the blessed moment when we shed the last vestige of self-delusion. All we can do is let this horrible moment of Peripeteia crash upon us like a merciless wave, pulling us down and threatening to drown us. Many of us succumb at this wave with mindless activity, drink, drugs, or flight. But our highest call is to endure the pain and stretch out on the cross of it. At that point, blessings come. We see and know or begin to know God. It is the losing our life to gain our life that Christ taught about."

Chief turned away from Madam with a disgusted look on his stressed countenance. Chairs scraped the floor as those remaining at Hazeltine's rose from the table and prepared to enter into the night. Madam Gardenia escorted her patrons through the now empty public dining room to the front door. Alton, Jerry, the judge, and the doctor boarded the limo for a return to the Peabody. Bobby left with the fan's wife in her Mercedes convertible. Raven appeared out of the shadows with an expression of low cunning and accompanied Chief down the hill toward the Father of Waters.

Chief and the Raven crossed the footbridge to

Desoto Island and continued to the tip of the island.
The dark trek took them through the rank miasma of
the islands tarn where a festival was to take place on the
following day. Overcome with his incipient delirium,
Chief sat cross legged in the sand and stared silently at
the dark flowing waters. He meditated for a period while
Raven hummed long improvised dirges. Finally Chief
stood and muttered, "Invisible is the only reality." With
these words upon his lips he walked into the swirling
river and yielded up his life. At the same time, Madam
Gardenia finished a letter to Chief and prayed for him.
Bobby rolled off the fan's wife and began snoring. Jerry
went to bed encouraged that the world was changing for
the better and everyone would be cared for. Alton slept
fitfully burdened instinctively with the knowledge that
times were changing rapidly and would never again be
the same. Raven walked back up the hill to the Peabody
started his bike and rode off into the darkness, knowing
his job was done.

The sun arose with a sickly yellow luster. Jerry and
Alton went to the coffee shop to begin their day. Sipping
coffee Jerry uttered, "Well I think Chief had a good
birthday day, don't you?"

Alton questioned, "Where is he? All I know is I saw
them walking last night down the hill toward the river."

Jerry poured more coffee. "I am most fond of Chief
but that old blackguard with him is too far gone."

Bobby got off the elevator and entered the coffee
shop. "Chief didn't come in last night but Madam
Gardenia sent him a letter. A bellman brought it up just
now. I opened it accidently. I thought it was for me but
here it is."

All three noticed through the coffee shop windows a
commotion down by the river. Police lights were flashing,
and a truck with sound equipment was being unloaded.
Jerry called, "Waitress we're ready to order, but what is
that going on down there on the island?" She took her
pencil from behind her ear and said, "They are setting up
the Mud Island Music Festival for this weekend. The Dixie
Flyers and Jim Dickerson are the headliners."

Alton asked, "Well what's that ambulance doing?
Bobby looked. "Wait, there's a wrapped body being

carried. That's not part of the music festival. Something's going on here."

The coffee shop was crowded and noisy but Alton could hear a police radio squawking. He looked at the next table where a police officer was eating with Memphis mayor Wyeth Chandler and an aide. The radio stopped squelching and Bobby, who had meet Chandler at various functions, asked, "What happened Mayor?"

The Mayor replied, "Oh good morning Bobby, I didn't notice you over there. A man drowned last night, I can't give you his name but he used to play football. He went in the river where Elvis skied."

Stunned, Alton took the letter from Bobby and read it aloud,

> *Dear Chief,*
>
> *The turning of the season is here. I pray and hope that you find that tender moment beyond rage and pain where G is waiting for you. Things are not as they should be in our world or our lives. By all means, we have a right to question the divine, but don't expect answers. The highest road before you is to let your faith endure. Don't live in mourning, don't sink into apathy, don't let the days of darkness prevail, weep but wipe the tears away. None of us have the ability to fix the world or even to understand. Our job is live without an answer but still live! Our abandonment gives us a blessing; we know who we are and we grow from that point. Along with the terror of being alone comes a realization of the gift we have, the gift of life and love. Then we emerge from our tunnel and face the dawn. Remember morning comes!*
>
> *Love*
> *Madam Gardenia*

Bobby spooned grits into his mouth. "Some swim, some sink, no matter. Waitress, more coffee please." The diners stared with empty eyes at the ambulance as it pulled slowly off the island and up the levee toward Chickasaw Bluff.

photo by Les Keller

Seldom if Ever

Rook, I'm told you died last Wednesday. They said you
were cleaning your trunk and pulled your 7mm rifle out
by the barrel and shot yourself. You crossed the Jordon
immediately; I believe that. Your son, Deuce, found you
a couple of hours later. Our esteemed coroner ruled the
death accidental; maybe it was. They said they tried to
reach me; maybe they did. You were cremated. Well many
choose that route now; it is cheaper by a long shot. You
were buried Saturday out by your dad Delepsis and your
brother Rice. No, the cemetery was not flooded. Spring
river rise aside, if that old cemetery was under water most
of North America would be inundated.

Rook, I am struggling to figure out what you
represented to me during the brief time we ran together.
For whatever reason, you were a star in a world to which
I was barred. Yes, you were a hometown river boy, but
your athletic skills, your fast cars, your girl friends were
most impressive to one who had none of these things.
In retrospect, I think what it was about you that appealed
to most of us was your level of nonchalance. Even with
the things that happened to you, you never seemed to
get upset or fret. I give you credit. You surfed your wave
successfully for a long time. You were in full flow while
many of us ebbed, myself included; life is like that ain't

93

it bro. You never judged me and Likewise I won't judge
you. But I know now that neither of us ever did belong. I
thought you did but I know now how wrong I was.

Our neighborhoods were separated by a sewage
ditch; we called them bayous. One day your gang came
across the bayou to strike our high ground trenches at
the giant Oak. It was reminiscent of Pickett's charge at
Gettysburg or the Aussies at Gallipoli. Your attack squad
was composed of a fatherless Lebanese boy, two doctor's
sons, one lawyer's boy, and a malcontent. We resisted with
the male children of a judge, a lawyer, an insurance crook,
a banker, and a Catholic boy from a broken home.

Our resistance was successful due to the fact that
one of our boys could sling a mud ball at great speed; in
fact, he had knocked our dentist's daughter out the week
before from a considerable distance. After we ran y'all
back across the bayou, we danced in victory under the
old oak while giving names to our little penises: fire hose,
lodge pole, stump, and Willapenapump. The son of the
insurance crook refused to participate in the naming.

Soon after our victory your father committed
suicide. I never saw you again until high school, but every
day I would see your mom passing up Chambers Street.
She was a striking woman. She would be on the way to the
Jitney Jungle or to teach art at Bowmar or maybe just to
get away. The windows in her car were always down; her
hair blew tall and bouffant and her sunglasses always hid
her tears.

You were a track star and most popular, but after
you found your father's body hanging limp, after his
suicide, you were different. You would stand in the hall
before class and dare anyone to hit you and try they did
but you were quick enough to dodge any and all blows.
Then when the bell rang you would do a flat standing
reverse flip and saunter into class. You dated anybody
you wanted to, and much to my chagrin, you won a dance
contest with Kari, a girl with whom I was infatuated.

You spent your senior year weighing offers for track
scholarships; you accepted an offer from Louisiana State
University. One weekend we hooked up when you came
to Ole Miss to stay with Ferris, my trailer mate. I was
stammering my way through law school, tripping over my

fur coat & carrying enough baggage to sink a city class ironclad. You had a muscle car and did not dress like the Ole Miss boys. True to form you still never seemed to care about anything. You dated a real live Ole Miss cheerleader. I liked your deal. Maybe admired is a better word. You were gentle with me; you never said anything about my full length faux fur coat or the half pint of Colonel Lee I carried in my pocket.

When you went to take your date back to campus, I rode with you. I didn't care for your car but thought maybe I could find out how you hooked up with a cheerleader. Your car had metal straps and chains that locked the hood down and a large hood scoop dominating the view from the windshield. You parked in front the Chi Omega house, walked your girlfriend to the porch and began kissing her fervently. I revved the motor in protest because my princess had left me a month before for a boy she later married and I wanted to express disdain for the culture that had busted my kudzu. The motor noise didn't bother you at all but the house mother and the returning coeds were most disdainful. Afterward, we joined Ferris and Chris Woods at Kiame's for a late snack. Returning to our mobile home park, we had to step over the football player who was passed out in a shallow snow bank near our trailer.

The following week my property professor called on me to explain a case we were examining. I stood and gave what could have been mistaken for a Sierra Club recording of a humpback whale in distress. The future governor sitting behind me and my other classmates averted their eyes; in my mind I had crashed and burned. Later that month, I received an award from my fellow law students because when leaving a law school party I accidentally ran my contracts professor off a gravel road. He and I met on a sharp curve and he swerved and lost control and crashed into the woods. I still have the award signed by all my classmates, "The Golden Thumb Got Cha" in gilded parchment. Needless to say, my reputation was spreading. The weekends eventually began in mid-week; a combination of emotional disorder, heartbreak and reality precipitated my dismissal from law school. I returned to my hometown somewhat depressed and lost.

You had graduated from undergraduate school and Likewise moved back to our home town. You had a farm implement business in Rolling Fork and farmed your family land up Highway 3. You and your new wife, the cheerleader, lived in an apartment across the hall from my girlfriend. Most of my friends were gainfully employed. Lamar was a salesman, Jonathan and his brother were attorneys, Baird was a doctor, and Ferris was handling casting for a film crew across the river. I was employed at the Old Southern Tearoom tending bar.

One night you and your wife and several other couples were in the bar and I began to take the trash out during a lull. One of my former law professors happened to be in town for a historical seminar. He was entering the bar while I was going out with the trash. He remembered me from his class and looked aghast. He asked me what I was doing. I stammered something about trash and he laughed and mentioned something about my papers being suitable for a similar destination. I was most irritated and embarrassed but you had him sit at your table and you told him that I was the owner of the Tea Room and that I did not have time for the legal profession and that he was a bona fide ass. I was grateful. Still it was tempting to consider taking my trot lines out of the water; whatever bait I was using wasn't working at all. I wasn't angry with the professor or anyone else. Just myself.

That fall you invited me to hunt at your camp with Jonathan, Lamar and the Angus boys. In between hunts, while y'all drank and played cards, I spent most of my time working on an outline for a story taking place at a camp in the Delta in which evil blacks and rednecks joined forces against the privileged class. Why not Rook? Yes! I was stuck and stalled and then some. But writing was the only way I could think of to move from ebb to flow. Knowing that I was different and rapidly becoming more so, my fellow huntsmen took it upon themselves to stick my unattended shotgun into the soft ground. The gesture filled a couple of inches of my barrel with buckshot mud. Then they set up a range and took me out to shoot on the pretense that I hadn't fired my gun yet. The barrel of my cheap shotgun exploded. They laughed uproariously; I didn't really care.

The Delta evening hue was purple as we made our

way back to town from the camp at twilight. We could see the lights of Goldie's coming on as we crossed the Mississippi River Bridge. Lamar was driving and Jonathan sat in the front seat; they offered a full load of Southern wisdom to me as I cradled my busted shotgun in the back seat. They lectured me that writing was a waste of time because I wasn't really steeped in literature. Staring blankly in the gathering dusk at the endless rows of cotton plants stripped of their bolls, I thought about what they said but it did not register.

Back at the apartment, my girlfriend was appalled at my literary efforts and the fact that I had not drank and gambled with the boys. It was the denouement; truth was, my idiosyncrasy had done us in. Within weeks she had begun to date one of your gang that had crossed the bayou to attack the giant oak. My position had become unsustainable. I took my trot lines up and pulled out. I eked out a living in Atlanta, New Orleans, Birmingham, Louisville, New York, Nashville, and Memphis. Still I wrote, but I found that I could not outrun what I was attempting to flee. For several years I did no better than the redneck poachers who crossed under my stand on that last hunt. Then one night in New Orleans, I dreamt my father's soul was leaving his body. It was the night in which he was stricken with a cerebral hemorrhage and my brother woke me up with the saddest news I had ever heard. My father was gone.

It was finally time to step up Rook; no more melancholy games. You seemed on top of the world when I left. When the casinos came to town, you bought Rachel's Kitchen from the man who used to run Darnel's. Ironically, at the same time you were negotiating with the owner, I was contacting his son, a producer in Hollywood. I was seeking an entree that never came; maybe your entree never came either. You never let on but I could sense that you were lost and pained when I saw you several years later at Maxwell's. My long process of healing had begun and your decline had started. You had left your wife and married Lamar's wife. Even with a new wife, the long hours at your failing restaurant left time only for your mistress, a waitress in your business. But, she cost you a brother. She was your brother's girl and he caught you with her late one night at Fort Hill. He killed himself later that evening over in Mounds. You found him three days later, rotted in the summer oven of the cab of his pickup. No one ever knew what the note he left for you said.

After Rice's death, I never saw you again. Rachel's Kitchen closed; you moved to your wife's family land east of the river so she could at least have the consolation of being near her aging mom. You continued consorting with your mistress for a time until her brother finally squired her away from you and gave her a job on the gulf coast with his garbage concern.

So it is over my brother. But we both know something that most of us seldom if ever realize. We, all of us, are treading 7mm's away from eternity. Rook, you have ebbed and by God's grace I am finally flowing. Even though I haven't seen you in over thirty years and will never see you again, I'll miss you ... in fact, I loved you more than you know.

Rest in peace Rook! God will sort it out! Rest in peace!

Early Camellias

"I returned, and saw under the sun that the race is not to the swift, nor the battle to the strong, neither yet bread to the wise, nor yet riches to men of understanding, nor yet favor to men of skill, but time and chance happen to them all. For man also knoweth not his time: as the fishes that are taken in an evil net, and as the birds that are caught in the snare, even so are the sons of men snared in an evil time, when it falleth suddenly upon them."—Ecclesiastes 9:11-12

The late morning was damp and chilled like the inside of a meat locker. The delivery man pulled up to the office trailer behind the funeral home. He knocked on the busted screen door. In his hands he gripped three white bags with the hideous countenance of a hog's head on the side. It was the usual order: triple meat, fries, and coke. The coroner's office was in a mobile home. The thin paneled wall behind the coroner's desk had a calendar from the local pool hall, a clock from the First Baptist Church, and an outdated schedule for the local football team.

The office was composed of one large room with two desks and a couch. Between the secretary's desk and the couch was placed a cheap coffee table with a stack of brochures entitled "Total Care in Your Time of Need." A hallway led to restrooms and a spare room where certain unmentionable autopsy tools were kept. The tall secretary was overdressed and chewing gum. She wore three-inch heals and a little leather skirt with large flowers on it and a tight sweater. Her tresses of jet black hair accented her natural lasciviousness.

"In or out Bubba, it's cold this morning." She let the man in and took the food. The screen door slammed. She carried the bags of food to the coroner's desk and paid Bubba, who left immediately. There was another knock on the screen door; she ran back to answer, almost tripping over the feet of the man slumped on the couch.

A man in a blue uniform with several spots of dried blood on his pants and his name over the front shirt pocket said, "Two bodies out here for y'all. One a plane crash and one walked into a propeller or something."

"Ok, Ok let me get this barbecue taken care of. Hey boss! Your order is here."

The director called from the adjacent restroom while washing his hands. "Ah breakfast! You are truly praiseworthy madam. I am full of affection for you and yours."

Ignoring her boss, she asked the man, "You got any paper work?"

He handed the crumpled papers to her and inquired, "Where's your restroom?" She motioned down the hall with a nod of her head as she examined the papers. The trailer bounced and shuddered as the man walked down the hall toward the john. She thought of how many times she had asked the county to level the trailer with no response. After using the restroom the man brought the bodies in and collected the papers that the secretary had filled out and then he left.

Even though there were few other cars in the lot, the preacher parked his old sedan in the spot reserved for pastors. It was a habit he couldn't break. When he got out, the driver's seat, which was propped up by a boat paddle, fell backward. He reached in the car and retrieved his stained topcoat; he put it on even though the walk to the coroner's office was short. He slammed the dusty car door and walked toward the office. His sensible shoes made no sound on the moist concrete. He entered the building as the secretary handed the papers to her boss who had just walked into the room wiping his hands. His suit was neatly pressed and expensive, his shoes shined and Italian, his weight over 400 pounds. He looked at the papers and laid them on the desk and began to read them. "Titus and that new young businessman. What a shame."

The secretary walked back to her desk; the man on the couch watched her listlessly. Doc looked pale. His body sunk into the deep divan as if he were surrounded by coffin cushions. He was for all appearances a wasted, broken soul. His eyes were watery and horribly revulsed; his clothing rumpled and disheveled. He took a long nip from a silver flask and wiped his mouth. He began to talk to the secretary as she shuffled papers on the desk. "I was a little worried about Titus that night; he seemed tired. I caught him in the urinal after midnight weeping some about his little girls; but he kept going like always. He woke me up crowing like a rooster off the balcony of the Monteleone at 6:30 a.m." The secretary looked at him with a quizzical glance. He continued. "It's a morning routine. We've done it many times. Crow at dawn, vomit, beignet and coffee, B-12; then back to the airport for the flight back to home and hearth." He lowered his head and began shedding tears. "This time I took a cab back up here. I wasn't about to fly with him."

The secretary sighed, "I know Doc. I'm sorry about your friend, but it saved your life." Answering the phone and turning to the man behind her, she said, "Boss, it's the deputy from down there."

He lifted the phone from his desk and placed the receiver to his ear. "Good morning sir. Just tell me what happened so I can put it in my coroner's report."

The deputy's voice crackled. "I was at the store, just got my lunch and was standing on the porch. First thing I heard was the airplane's motor gunning like a car trying to get out of a ditch. I could see the plane not far away, seen it clear. It was pretty low in the sky. I could even read the registration numbers. Then it started jumping and shaking and the wing come off."

The coroner sat down and placed a notebook on the edge of his desk. "Slow down now son I can't write that fast."

The deputy repeated, "The wing come off and the

cabin started spinning and falling. I called HQ on my radio then ran over there behind the store. Have you ever tried to run in a plowed field? It's hard. I fell once cause I was trying to keep my hat on and my boots was slick."

Rolling his eyes at his secretary, the boss said, "No, I've never had to run in a field officer, but go ahead."

The deputy continued. "One of the engines was right behind the store; some other broken stuff was scattered around. I couldn't find the cabin at first. There wasn't any smoke or fire, just dust. I seen some broken trees and I ran over there. The cabin was in the woods just banged up some and still intact. Some local kids were already there and we looked in the cockpit windows. The man was just lying back in his seat, his neck was at an odd angle, and his sunglasses were sort of twisted on his face. A little blood trickled out of his nose, his coat had been ripped and his glasses was busted. You could tell he was gone; we knew it right away.

The coroner finished writing and said, "Thank you Deputy; send me the report if you would." He hung the phone up and looked up from signing the papers. "Greetings Pastor. How'd you find out? I was just about to call you." Waving magnanimously at the white bags with the hogs head visage, the coroner said, "How about some barbecue?"

The minister sat on the divan near Doc, his pre-Easter felt hat in his hands. He waved the offer of food away. "I got a call from his wife. She is pretty torn up, and I'm on the way out there now."

Chewing a mouthful of hot pork and French fries, the coroner opined, "Well I knew it was coming. I knew he wouldn't die in his bed out at the house. You learn to read these things. It's like a boil coming under the levee before it breaks. You find it if you look."

The clergyman looked down thoughtfully. "I liked the man. He had a nice family and his business seemed to be doing well. He had a good heart, but like many of us he was in conflict."

Opening another sandwich, the coroner said, "Conflict? Bull Preacher! He was a man approaching middle age, fatter than me, and he was having a come apart. Everybody knows he had a gal friend in New Orleans."

Seemingly unoffended, the minister fiddled with his collar. "Well, he was under some sort of pressure and you could tell it. He hadn't been at church as much lately but he still sent in his tithe and his wife and the girls came every Sunday. I saw him at Rotary Club."

"Dammit! I spilled sauce all over my tie," The coroner cursed. "I'm gonna have to start keeping these ties in the fridge so they won't spoil!" Wiping the stained tie with his hanky he said, "Did y'all hear what Titus did three nights ago at the King Edward hotel in Jackson? He and his lawyer's little brother got after that fullback from Ole Miss from a few years back and really cleaned his plow. The fullback wound up getting arrested; he started it anyway. I wouldn't be afraid to go up against anybody with that kid on my side!"

Doc roused from his lethargy on the couch and took another pull on the flask. He wiped his mouth on his suit sleeve and muttered, "My tankard is now empty!" On the couch beside Doc, the pastor turned to examine him more closely. Doc continued speaking to no one in particular. "Titus had all those elective surgeries over the past few years. I know he hurt; we could all see it. He told me that car seats really hurt him and he couldn't get comfortable in a car so he flew everywhere he could. He hurt his back at Mississippi State playing football and it never got right. After the fourth operation he relied on the pills."

The secretary turned from her filing while listening to Doc's lament. "If he hadn't had that plane ..." Her voice trailed off.

"You are right my dear," opined Doc. "I should compose a madrigal to you." The preacher looked at him quizzically. Doc continued. "He did as he pleased and not many of us can do that. When drunk, which was often, his favorite phrase was ... I best not repeat it. Sometimes when Titus wanted me to go on a trip with him he would call the office and just play his blender. Nothing else was needed; my receptionist knew what was afoot. She would call and cancel my afternoon appointments. I would give her a few bucks to go shopping at the Valley Department store and I would meet him at the airport. He mostly called when we were going to some little town near New Orleans or Memphis so we could just hop over the line in his plane when he was finished. I guess I would have gone anywhere when he called but my wife started giving me hell and one of my patients had an abscess and almost died so I cut back some."

Leaning back on the couch and frowning disapprovingly at the other man, the preacher said, "Off course, I saw him in the hospital after every operation. I tried to catch up with him several times at his office but he was out of town every time I did."

The coroner had finished all three sandwiches alone and was now putting everything in the waste basket beside his desk and draining his coke. "Well brace yourself Preacher. This funeral will be one of those occasions where someone dies at the height of power and influence and everyone in town who is in business comes; it will be packed, standing room only. We've already received many calls from staff in his stores. The secretary nodded. If he had died twenty years from now the crowd would have been half as large. By the way Reverend, I've been to your church. You ain't used to preaching in front of so many people, are you?"

II

The long drive up to the Titus house was lined by camellia bushes. The once massive grounds were now reduced to a narrow lawn with a long drive that adjoined to the national military park. Three cannons and a statue of a Union officer who fought at Vicksburg had been placed on a berm within sight of the front door. Other homes had gradually encroached upon the grounds over the years and the once magnificent house was now part of a normal neighborhood on the edge of the military park. Last night's storm had left a sheen of ice on the windows and the trees. The first rays of the winter sun shone on the white brick home and the patina of icy moisture made the old mansion look as if it were newly painted. Only two lights were on, one upstairs and another downstairs. Smoke trailed from the massive chimney located on the side of the house. No sounds were coming from within.

Inside huge logs crackled in the kitchen fireplace as

two young girls settled in to breakfast. The sleepy mother was at the stove. "Damn these old mansions," Titus thought. "No insulation, small bathrooms, hardly room to move and not enough electric plugs." Splashing cold tap water on his face, he thought, "Thank the Lord the ghost was quiet last night. I needed sleep after the King Edward incident." He shaved, quickly, put on his best Hickey-Freeman suit and his brown wingtips and thought to himself, "I need to go down to Karl's and get a couple of new suits and fresh ties." Coming down the spiral staircase, he heard voices in the kitchen and smelled coffee. He walked quietly through the dark ball room adjacent to the kitchen. Every time he went through the room he tried to remember what the occasion for the famous ball that took place at the house in 1862 had been. He vaguely remembered a Federal admiral had run the gauntlet of Confederate cannons on the river front and it was announced at the ball. Was it Porter or Farragut? He never could recall. No matter.

He entered the kitchen. His wife was at the stove stirring grits and his daughters sat sleepily at the big table. Walking up behind the woman in the faded flannel nightgown, he asked, "Did you let those curs out yet?"

"Yes, I did. Yesterday. And they just now came home; those dogs are just like you. They run and roam all night long."

Pouring a cup of coffee, Titus replied, "Yeah, well don't worry about it." The two rangy hounds rested by the flickering fire licking their paws and smiling up at him. He patted the dog's heads. "At least I bring something home; here is your check!"

Putting food on the little girl's plates, she answered, "Put it over by the phone. What time did you get in from Jackson last night?" She spoke but her eyes never left the stove.

He averted his eyes. "The meeting went late at the King Edward. I told you that."

"Breakfast! Come on girls!"

The two little girls ran forward for the plates. Watching the little ones, Titus said, "I'll eat at the Tea Room."

Turning from the stove and looking at him for the first time, she said, "I hate that plane, but at least you'll be home before the girl's play on Friday."

"Yes Daddy! Please!" the girls wailed in unison.

Smiling at them he said, "Oh, I wouldn't miss it little ladies. No way!" Bending, he kissed his sleepy daughters. "See you Friday ladies."

His wife stopped him as he turned. "Wait Titus. You cut yourself shaving; let me get the blood before it gets on your clothes. Those managers will be rolling dice for your coat if I don't." After wiping his face, she walked with him through the dark house to the front door. Opening it, she shivered in the dawn chill. They stepped over the threshold out onto the porch; she gathered her robe around her tightly. A single bird chirped from its nest in the porch eves. Next to the walk, the camellias were beginning to bud. Turning away, she looked at the trees lining the drive and was mesmerized at how they shimmered in the pale sunlight. "I hope this unseemly weather doesn't hurt my early camellias." His dutiful kiss ended her somber reverie. He walked off the porch and disappeared into the early morning shadow. She stepped back in and pushed the door shut and watched him go up the drive from the little side window adjacent to the door. Walking back through the darkened ball room, she called out, "We're running late girls, time for school now."

He drove down the drive past the statue of the bronze soldier and his horse and turned towards the town square. He rounded the curve and passed the Sisters of Mercy Convent. Some of the convent lights were on and the Sisters of Mercy were up, early as usual, praying. As he rounded the curve into town, he thought of his wife's aunt who resided in the convent; "Sister," he muttered "say one for me." He stopped at the River City News Stand for *The Ledger, The Picayune* and *The Appeal*. He parked at the Tea Room, gathered his newspapers, exited his car and entered the restaurant. Two other customers ate sullenly at separate tables. He nodded to them. One was a delivery driver; the other was a local nut case lawyer. The driver nodded back; the lawyer ignored him. A large waitress watched him come in; she was dressed like Aunt Jemimah. She greeted him absentmindedly and thrust a menu at him. Waving the menu away, he said, "I don't need that. Is Miss Mary up yet?"

"No sir, she's a little ill this morning."

Titus laughed, "Well what else is new? Poor baby!

When is she gonna learn that the cordial she sips on all day is not good for her? I'll have the stuffed ham, silver dollar biscuits, and grits." Then, winking at the waitress, he added, "And when you have time, bring me a touch of that medicine you keep back there for Miss Mary." The waitress ignored him like she did every morning and took his order back to the kitchen where the old chef waited beside his stove. While waiting for his breakfast, Titus perused the papers trying to get a weather report for New Orleans in anticipation of his trip.

The sky had begun to clear when he reached the municipal airport. He parked, straightened his tie, smoothed his suit, put his aviator glasses on and made sure his hair was in place. As he entered the terminal building, the airport manager was already unhappy about something or other. He was on his second cigar and deep into his first pot of coffee. He growled, "That mobile home manufacturer just took off and his fat ass plane is too big for my runway." Handing the phone receiver to Titus, he said "It's your damn secretary and your attorney has called already. Your passengers, that broken down dentist and the young buck insurance man are in the waiting room. I'm tired of keeping your schedule for you."

Titus took the phone. "Relax old man. You ain't on that aircraft carrier anymore." He placed the receiver to his ear. "Hello little lady."

The secretary said, "Boss, you have the store audit from Mint Springs and Panther Burn before noon, the mid-afternoon grand opening in Bogue Chita, and the awards ceremony for managers at the Commanders Palace in New Orleans."

Titus smiled as he listened. "Ok Sugar, I got it covered, they're getting my chariot ready now."

Ignoring him, she continued. "Oh and your attorney called to say he won't be flying with you this morning. He said to let you know that he would drive down and meet you at Commanders."

Glancing at his watch, Titus said, "That poor barrister don't know what he is missing. It's heaven up there!"

Doc and the young businessman had come out of

the waiting room. The younger man looked quizzically
at the laughing Doc who was telling him that after a few
more flights he would qualify for his own hot water bottle
so he could piss while they were still in the sky. Grinning
regally as the two approached, Titus said, "Greetings,
gents. I will have my swing low sweet chariot towed out of
its hanger for us. We have places to go and people to see."
The airport manager scowled and called the hanger.

It was twilight in New Orleans; the runway lights had just
come on, gentle whitecaps rose and fell on Lake Ponchartrain. Three women sat in the waiting area on cheap fake
leather couches with shiny metal arms. They thumbed
through outdated magazines. They were dressed for an
evening out. The oldest of the three exuded an elegance
that was alluring and very handsome. She was possessed of
a certain faded beauty with a loveliness that spoke of the
poignant magic of ruins. Her brown eyes had a fascinating
power. She was a former dancer now working as manager
at Titus's New Orleans store. The second woman appeared
to have had some acquaintance with the first. The wife of
a classics scholar at Tulane University, she was thin, short,
and girlish. She fancied herself to be a darkling sorceress
and was well versed in the ancient art of New Orleans'
dark spirituality.

   The third had never been with the other two ladies.
She was married to a commercial fisherman and had a
fresh tattoo of a pelican above her ankle. Brash, swarthy,
and loud, she was most attractive and most unhappily
married. She was not remarkable for her intelligence or
her kindness. Gingerly rubbing the new tattoo on her leg,
the third woman said, "I'm sore. It still hurts some. I don't
know why I did it. I just can't wear these high heels with
this new tattoo. Now, tell me again, who are these men?"

   The older woman replied, "They come about three
times a year. It's fun. When we met, I was still working at
Mason Blanche and waitressing on the Lakefront part time.
Now I work for him."

   "What do you do for him?" asked the third lady, still
rubbing her tattoo.

   "I manage his store up on Carrollton Avenue."

   The second woman looked around. She had been

gazing at the runway lights flaring in the twilight. "Look, we go eat. It's nothing serious. Mandinas, Pascal Manales, and tonight the Commander's Palace. We go listen to jazz, sometimes we even shop on Canal."

The third woman blurted, "Do you ever go to bed with them?"

Laughing brusquely, number two said, "Lil' Pelican, that's none of your business. I'm married."

The older woman got off the couch and walked toward the window, coming in between the two women. "Sometimes if we feel like it we stay with them but it's not any big deal."

The second woman turned back toward the window. "It's not about that for me. It's about getting out of the house. My husband is writing a book and he is hard to get along with."

The older woman added, "We never know exactly when they are coming. They will call in the afternoon and if we can we come out here and pick them up. The one I'm with, Titus, has a bunch of stores. The other guy is a doctor of some kind I think."

The third woman put her sore ankle up on the coffee table and asked, "What about the third guy?"

Laughing, the second woman said, "Oh he's a cheerleader at LSU, wouldn't you like that Lil' Pelican?" The third woman scowled at her but made no comment. Walking back over to the couch the second woman attempted to smooth ruffled feathers. "But they have plenty of money, let me tell you, and they ain't afraid to let it go."

Smiling now, the older woman said, "Remember last time? We went down to the Quarter to meet some musician Titus knew from Dr. Ferris's house in Vicksburg and the guy didn't even remember him."

"Yeah but he got in such a mood," the second chimed in. "He was not as funny that night and nobody had a good time."

"Yes it was quite a night," sighed the first. "We were in Jackson Square that night and wanted to have our portraits made. The painter did ours but wouldn't do one of Titus, even after Titus flashed his roll at him."

All three rose and stood looking out at the Pontchartrain as the plane began its final approach to the airport. It crossed the lake and angled over the river for the landing. On board the aircraft in daylight's final moments the three men could see the Crescent City sprawling warm and inviting. They were anxious to land. It had been a long day. Mint Springs, Panther Burn, and Bouge Chitto had been excruciatingly boring. They were looking forward to seeing the women. Titus and the Doc, having made this trip many times, had used their hot water bottles several times to relieve themselves, but the youngest man, new to the protocol, had to piss really badly. During the final leg from Bouge Chitto, he had refused offers of use of their bottles. They touched down on the runway nearest the lake and came toward the terminal. It was getting dark quickly. The women saw the lights of the plane and got up and walked outside the waiting room to the little patio where passengers disembarked. The three stood behind a chain link fence. The plane taxied towards the spot near where the three women stood.

Doc spotted the women standing behind the fence and waxed eloquently from the co-pilots seat. "How beautiful they would be in elaborate and stately court dresses, descending the marble steps of palaces, opposite great lawns and fountains, seen through the atmosphere of a lovely night."

The plane wheeled and stopped, the props still running; fiddling with various controls in the cockpit, Titus laughed, "Get real Doc. It's only a business trip and a little extra."

Undaunted, Doc crowed, "The clowns have arrived to greet their queens."

The young man squirmed. "Man, y'all hush. I got to piss bad. Hurry up will you." He unhooked his seat belt before the plane stopped by the gate and uttered, "I got to see a man about a dog."

Leaning forward so the man could get out, Doc said, "Kid, next time we'll bring a hot water bottle for you; you've earned your wings."

The young business man hurried toward the gate and ran into the propeller. The prop made one very loud cracking bump then spun again. It had sliced him and tossed him away limp, broken, and dead. His body leaned against the fence in a sitting position, blood rapidly pooling under him. All three women had blood spatters in their shoes and hose. The sorceress, seemingly unperturbed, mopped up blood from her legs with a hanky. The other two stood frozen. Titus and Doc climbed out of the plane and stared in disbelief. Airport personnel and taxi drivers began to gather. The young man's body was now illuminated by the garish lights of the portico roof which had come on automatically at twilight.

Regaining his composure, Titus gathered the three upset ladies and signaled for a taxi. One pulled up almost immediately with a burly driver at the wheel. "Ladies, get in the cab and wait for Doc and me," Titus ordered. "We'll join you as soon as we answer questions and sign whatever needs to be signed." He turned to go into the terminal but came back and handed them a bottle. "Pray if you must or drink if you please; we'll be less than an hour dolls."

Forty-five minutes later Titus and Doc walked back out to the cab. Lil' Pelican complained, "Where are we going? I'm sick! There's blood all over my new tattoo."

The second woman said, "Relax! Blood from a violent death can be a powerful talisman." In the front seat, Titus ordered the driver, "Take us to the My Oh My Club. Ladies, we'll have cocktails and then go on to dinner."

As the cab pulled away, two uniformed men lifted the shattered body into a rubber bag.

Titus gave the driver a wad of crumpled bills and said, "Pick us up in an hour. We need to get up to Commander's for dinner. There's another couple hundred in it for you if you stick with us and carry us back out to Lake Front Airport in the morning."

When the taxi arrived at Commander's Palace the company attorney greeted them at the curb. A chill was creeping in off the River. Titus hurried everyone into the building. Managers and their wives were beginning to arrive. Most of the women immediately sought the restroom where they re-arranged and primped all the while watching new arrivals in the mirror. The men seemed nervous but pleased to be in the inner sanctum of the company. They admired the ice carving and picked at shrimp while they waited for their wives.

The old banquet captain stood silently against the wall fingering his luxurious, white handlebar mustache; his wise eyes were filled with a "seen it all look." He watched his people make final preparation for the banquet. Waiters stood at the edge of the room. Titus approached the banquet captain who nodded in recognition. "Whatever my people need captain!" The old captain signaled and immediately waiters came to life bearing trays of green and silver cocktails that matched Titus' company's logo. Most guests were hesitant at first but soon they relaxed and descended like locusts on the bar and the groaning board of food. The set-up was decadent in its extravagance; it contained all the gumbo, crayfish, and shrimp one could consume and enough champagne to float the Mississippi Queen. Everything was displayed beautifully on antique tables.

After the proper period of libation, Titus took the microphone and greeted the managers most cordially. When he announced the grand opening of the new store in Bogue Chito, applause was scattered. After thanking all the managers and their wives, he announced manager of the year and presented the manager from the store in Picayune with a painting of the store and tickets for a trip upriver onboard the Delta Queen for the winner and his wife. Then he announced, "Now the moment, for which you have been waiting, our featured guests who have had a seminal influence on the music of our day. May I present for your listening pleasure, New Orleans recording artist Dr. Piano and the Spleens." The little red curtain parted and a cadaverous old man with gold teeth, dime store sunglasses and a cape was assisted to the baby grand by two members of his band. Dr. Piano immediately began to play. The sound was infectious; jovial drinkers formed a conga line and slithered through the room. Managers and wives alike joined in the wild, unabashed celebration. Titus and the company lawyer mingled with the guests who stood watching the conga line. They moved from group to group on the side; sometimes joining conversations, sometimes not, but always speaking and shaking hands.

One manager's wife was overheard telling another, "We saw a woman in the quarter this afternoon that had more body hair than a rangatang. She stood outside the Famous Door Club combing herself with a red comb and collecting whatever coins people threw." The other replied, "Do whatever you gotta do girl!"

A flush faced, portly man in a plaid sport coat spoke to the company attorney. "Isn't she a precious jewel?"

"You mean the she devil with the pelican tattoo? I would lie if I did not confess that I immediately found in her a bizarre charm."

The portly man continued. "I hear you always drive down. Why won't you fly with the boss?"

The lawyer sighed as if he had heard the question before and explained, "It's his plane. The model that Titus flies is a death trap. They were made in Oklahoma beginning in 1951. Our company has the economy version 500 which was introduced in 1958. It is basically a stripped down 560 with the same problems. The main problem is that both the 500 and the 560 are susceptible to stress fatigue which leads to metal cracking, especially in the wing spars and numerous crashes have happened as a result. Our company plane has twin 250 hp Lycoming O-540-A engines; only a hundred were built. Titus bought it used from some rock and roll player in Memphis for eighty five thousand and thought he had a bargain."

Gobbling another shrimp the man said, "Well, I believe when it is your time it is your time no matter what."

Bored, the lawyer looked away and muttered, "No sense hurrying it along."

The man looked away disgustedly. "You sound like a lawyer."

The lawyer smiled. "I am! But those planes have continued to fall out of the sky at an alarming rate." The man grabbed another handful of shrimp and wandered along to join the conga line.

Nearby another manager admired the Tulane professor's wife. "Did you see that little one? She is an enchantress, a Venus."

His friend replied, laughing, "I'll bet she has some demands in her that can't be met—money, attention, and whatever. Once she gets a hold on a man it's all over."

The other spoke over the music, "It might be worth it Bubba! But I like the Pelican girl better."

Titus moved toward the bar while telling a manager his secret for working such long hours. "It's because I played football that my body can take the punishment. But the key is my plane. That's how I get it done; I save time." The first woman was sitting to the side; she spoke quietly with other guests. The little sorceress bounced through the room like an irritated reptile and Pelican girl sat surrounded by three corpulent men seeking her favor.

A man wearing gumbo all over his shirt and quaffing a drink said to a colleague, "Buddy, I've learned! My partner partied until 8 a.m. after the Sugar Bowl. He finally went to bed; he awoke 2 hours later with chest pain and shortness of breath and by the time his girlfriend could get help he was dead and gone at 34. He left a wife and two kids."

Sipping his drink, Doc entered the conversation. "He obviously planned to fall like Icarus into legend. Did it did not occur to him that Icarus had fallen unnoticed upon the unyielding crust of a busy world?" Doc laughed at his own wit and impudently showed teeth remarkably bad for a dentist. His enormous idiotic laugh rang through the room like that of men the world over after they have dined too well and had too much to drink.

When the affair came to a close, Titus thanked everybody for coming, congratulated the manager of the year once more and watched as the group began to depart. Several of the long term managers were going to meet Titus in his suite at the Monteleone Hotel. After the last couple left the Commander's Palace, Titus paid off the banquet captain and stepped outside; the cab was waiting. Lil' Pelican had left earlier with one of the managers but Titus and Doc and the other two women went to the Monteleone suite reserved for them. Late night winter darkness enveloped the French Quarter; a cold wind blew from the West Bank. A large freighter moved slowly upriver with lights ablaze.

Titus' girlfriend sat alone on the balcony with her rosary. Titus eventually joined her; he plopped next to her and rubbed his eyes. "I am tired." For a brief moment his eyes exposed the languor of his heart, but he caught himself quickly. "Let me get you a taxi and you can ride up and down Bourbon Street in your nightgown throwing gold coins to your subjects."

"Did you call his wife?" she asked curtly.

"Our lawyer got through to her before we left Commander's," Titus replied. He looked out over the river. "I've had a rough two weeks. I need to slow down."

"You're running from something, and you can't escape. With your perpetual disquietude, all the honors, all the money that anyone could confer won't ever be enough for you." Titus glared at her but didn't have the energy to engage. Looking away from him, she continued. "In the midst of all our careening about it is sad to see how every creative work of God except people gives praise to him. And yet, God's work goes on; the bird sings, the flowers bud. Why do we mock God in our flailing about?" He sat quietly, his face showing no signs of response. "All is fair and lovely and in perfection except our troubled spirits. This hour is a parable of the dark threshold we have crossed, a world where the darkening has suddenly leaped upon us. But look at the moonlight, the quiet French Quarter filled with palm trees shimmering in soft light and then look at us."

At this Titus flared. "*Please* stop preaching."

"I worry about your health," she replied softly. "You exhaust yourself. Why don't you stop, move down here, find a little house that is simple, settle down and relax?"

He moved his foot quickly in an attempt to get the large cockroach that had crossed the balcony on its nightly rounds. The roach scurried away. "Look, I see the world as it really is. That's why I can get things done. My company is making sufficient progress; it provides what I need for now."

She got to her feet and stood against the railing. A horse whinnied in the street below where the carriages were lined up. A couple entered the lead carriage and it pulled away from the hotel and plop-plopped down the empty street. Watching the departing carriage, she said, "You may not realize it, but your importunities cause grave injuries. In less than one year you have defiled your wife, your mistresses, your children, and now your friend is in the morgue. That young man worshiped you and you know it."

Titus stood. "Listen, I can't go to the race track tomorrow. My daughter has a play and I have to be back in Vicksburg. Will you tell the other girls?"

She backed away. "What is it that you want anyway?"

"Money!" replied Titus without smiling. "My goal is simple. Get rich."

Looking away from him and gazing across the river, she said, "How we honor and indulge our businessmen. Their sins and tirades are excused; it is seen as part and parcel of their management skills. But a price will be paid for our indulgence. For all the permission given you must create wealth and money."

Shifting in the cold wind, he sighed, "You don't understand; you've never really understood me. You want to make a monk out of me, but I'm a businessman. I plunge ahead to find the new ways to make money. As long as I am not under a marble monument, I keep moving and making dough. I need rest true enough but I seek something necessary to me."

She turned around to face him. "What about the spiritual?"

He uttered a short derisive laugh. "What of it? I seek something else; I don't know what I want. I just know I need money for it whatever it is." She turned away from him. Titus sighed. "I feel so lonely sometimes. My babies are in bed for hours now, my wife is sleeping and here I stand. Like some poet said, 'after every debauchery one feels lonelier and more abandoned.'"

Turning to face him, she said, "That's just my point. Your debauchery has nothing to do with making money. It's just ... " searching for a word she paused. "Just senseless filth."

Omnipresent mist was thickening around the street lights. Titus took a pull on the bottle of champagne he was clutching. "Well three more stores open next week Princess. Aren't you proud?" She clutched her rosary to her chest and muttered a silent prayer. He acted as if he did not see.

When he awoke from his restless sleep, humidity permeated the suite. Doc vomited and wretched in the toilet. Almost against his will, Titus matriculated the foul labyrinth of the rooms; he breathed in the rancidity and desolation of his narrow world. Waste and debris from last night littered the suite, crawfish hulls, hardening bowls of bisque, darkened merlatons, empty bottles and full ashtrays. One manager still lay on the couch. A dead bouquet languished in its thin glass coffin; he drained a glass and lit up his first.

Down on the river bank the concrete seawall glistened like a massive tombstone in the dawn chill. Two bums huddled around a fire of driftwood, passing a bottle back and forth. One could hear the cry of gulls lost in the fog, the lapping of the river, and a car trying to start. Algiers old cathedral steeple stood quietly alone across the river. Titus found his pants. He trembled as if with palsy and fell backward while trying to put them on. His mistress got up to help and gave him café-a-lait. He drank it and continued dressing as he gobbled a beignet. His B-12 shot laid at the ready on the dresser. After the shot, he finished packing. As he began walking out of the suite he paused briefly beside his mistress, hugged her and told her that the lawyer had made arrangements to have the body brought back to Vicksburg and that Doc had decided to take a cab back to Vicksburg and was not flying back with him. He then left without kissing her and took the elevator to the lobby. He flung his bag into the open trunk of the taxi and got in the back seat. The taxi sped to Lakefront Airport with little French and American flags crackling on the front fenders.

Titus had the plane fueled; the prop was still covered with the young man's blackish blood from the previous evening's accident. Confronted with the permanence of the incident again, he shook his aching head. But, it was a most glorious day, the sun was resplendent, and he was anxious to take off. Once airborne he noticed visibility was superb, in fact it was clear for miles. North of New Orleans, the landscape appeared to be uninhabited. Even in late winter it was green and verdant. He flew over an occasional little town, noticed a crossroads store now and then and little tin roofs on hillsides with thin wisps of transparent smoke trailing up toward his speeding plane. Passing over Bouge Chito, he noticed with pride and satisfaction that cars were already parked in the parking lot of his new store.

His little bird continued under the splenetic cupola of the azure sky, but the depth of the sky began to dismay him. Its limpidity exasperated him. Vaguely he sensed that something was amiss. Over Natchez, he was certain that something was wrong with his plane. The atmosphere in the cockpit slowly took on a quality of danger and fatality.

Still he did not panic; he figured his flight time to the Vicksburg Municipal Airport. Uneasily he fingered his galluses and adjusted his sunglasses. He realized that he was gonna miss his girls play. He began to search the landscape for a place to put the plane down; he searched the lay of the land ahead of him frantically. It was not to be; coming in over a little store near the Natchez Trace the plane started bucking and shuddering. He could see the patrol car and the deputy standing on the store porch in a stiff straw cowboy hat. The deputy was looking up at him and opening a can of Vienna sausages. Two dogs sitting in the gravel nearby were counting on the deputy's largesse. A dusty sedan was pulling into the lot. The morning sun shone in Titus' eyes and glinted off his glasses. "Hell," Titus thought, "right back where I come from—a dusty little hamlet in the middle of nowhere." He squinted and pulled feverishly on the stick while pushing on the throttle but it was too late and too little. The wing was already falling off and the fuselage began spinning slowly before it hurtled to the earth and into the shadow we call death.

III

The minister drove out to Titus' former home one afternoon six months later. His steering wheel was hot to the touch. He drove up the long narrow drive, his tires grinding on the gravel. The statue and the cannons on the berm looked like they were actually shimmering in the heat. The yard was barren with the exception of the rows of camellias along the drive that desperately needed water. He walked onto the porch and rang the bell. The wife greeted him at the door.

"I heard you coming. Come on in Pastor. What can I get you?"

Entering the house he answered, "Nothing really, thank you." She escorted him into the parlor and offered him a seat in a chair under the ceiling fan. He spoke uncomfortably, fidgeting with hat he now held in his hands. "I know you were irritated with me for not doing your wedding but it had only been six months; I just couldn't marry y'all that soon."

"It's okay Pastor, really. I have a new life now. You know I don't think poorly of you, never have. You served Titus and the girls and me for many years."

The clergyman furrowed his brow with sincerity. "I do plenty of funerals but his really hurt me. I want you to know that."

She replied without smiling, "When we married he was a gentle good man. He was a good provider for us, no doubt about that. I never had to work anywhere, just stayed home with my girls. I have a lot to be grateful for." After a slight pause, she continued. "But, that damned plane; I hated that plane. I almost never saw him after he bought it. Once we flew with the girls back home to my mom's in Byhalia. I just hated it; I never went back up in it again."

An awkward silence ensued. Not knowing exactly what to say, he asked, "What happened to your yard? It used to be so well kept, so lovely."

Smiling now, she replied, "We're just so busy, but the main reason is that we're leaving this house and moving to a plantation in the lower Delta. Our new home is being renovated now." Silence again ensued. Uncomfortably the wife uttered, "I got the girls in school at All Saints." He didn't reply or question. They heard a car on the gravel drive outside; the sunlight glinted off the approaching windshield. Relieved, she cried, "Oh good! My husband is home."

The preacher could hear heavy steps as the husband thumped across the wooden porch. Titus' former lawyer entered, keys clanked on the sideboard. He greeted the minister. "Hello Pastor. Long time no see."

The minister replied, "How are you sir?"

"Couldn't be better, thank you."

"Your wife tells me that you are going to move."

The husband smiled at his wife. "Yes, we found a little place that had fallen into ruin in the lower Delta. Honey, would you get me a drink?" She dutifully left the room and the grating sound of a blender was heard. Continuing, the lawyer said, "Preacher, I know what you are thinking. But none of this is untoward. Titus was a sharp businessman, and we made good money working together."

The clergyman shifted uneasily in his chair. "You don't have to…"

The lawyer interrupted, "Hear me out, now Preacher." Walking over to a humidor, the lawyer continued. "We never had to borrow much. I guess we were lucky and in the right place at the right time."

Watching the lawyer cross the room as he unwrapped his cigar, the minister offered, "We call it divine providence."

The lawyer settled comfortably in his deceased partner's favorite chair and lit his cigar. "The hours he could put in … it was amazing how he did it. He binged on work. When we had five locations turning a profit, he bought the plane. It seemed like a good idea. We needed it and he could travel the state much easier and check on our stores. He was as good a partner as I could ever have wanted. He could go somewhere and be home at night with his family. That was the idea anyway." Exhaling a large puff of smoke, he continued. "As for us, we have a good life now. We bought some land in the Delta and I still have some investments and strip malls in town, the ones he and I had together." Looking over his shoulder, he called, "Honey! Where's my drink?"

The minister began the drive back to town. His heart weighed heavy. People were bound and determined to ignore what was offered to them, to crawl in darkness rather than walk in light. He drove slowly, attempting to sort his thoughts. He rounded the curve near the edge of the hill where the Sisters of Mercy Convent had been since before the Yellow Fever epidemic of a prior century. Sisters were crossing the lawn going to noon prayer. The old convent building was silhouetted against a vivid blue sky which cared little if at all. His old car started down the hill into town. "I've always loved this view," he thought. The river stretching out of sight in both directions, the little town nestled in the bend, the old steamer Sprague moored just north of the city. "This town is like all other towns," he thought. "Its people are in dire need and most don't even know it." Noticing his watch, he increased his speed slightly; his afternoon Bible study started in fifteen minutes.

William Calhoun Fisher

William, I remember the day in which you died. I was
finishing my doctorate project and had planned to come to
the hospital as soon as I finished, but my bro you finished
before I did. Your brothers asked me to give a eulogy
at the Sisters of Mercy Convent and I sadly accepted.
Numerous books have been written to enumerate the
misery of unhappy lives and untimely deaths. In many
ways you were able to rise above the conflict; therefore, I
will not add you to these mournful narratives because your
life and vicissitudes entitle you to a degree of compassion
from all of us.

In preparing your eulogy, I had so many thoughts
about you and your life. I thought of the weekend you
were home from Ole Miss with the Hickerson brothers,
who both played football for the Rebels and were heroes
of mine. I thought of when you lived in a rental home
behind Miss Johnson's mansion with your new wife and
a logging truck. I remembered your reaction when your
sister was chosen as Miss Ole Miss. There was so much to
sort through.

Bro you were of large stature, tall and thick with
Irish features. Your deportment was far from subtle;
you were like a Jerry Lee Lewis on steroids or Elvis in
the weight room. It seemed to me that you smiled often

but you were seldom provoked to laughter. You moved ahead. You left your logging truck and got a good job in North Mississippi. You were complex and deep and many distressful perplexities seemed to weigh upon you. You did not behave with great firmness or rigidity, yet your personality earned for you much esteem and admiration. William Calhoun, our heroes have often been no less remarkable for what they have suffered than for what they have achieved.

I never knew of an occasion in which you took advantage of weakness or attacked the defenseless. You never pushed or pressed on the fallen or disadvantaged and even though you did not attempt to extricate them from their misfortune you bestowed your good wishes upon them. Others whom I knew thought that you may have been obstinate in your resentment of those who had done you wrong. Those who took this view were of the opinion that you were petulant and contemptuous and thought that you more frequently reproached than thanked. Yes. When you were angry you spoke of the insolence and partiality of those you perceived to have wronged you. However, if that conduct is all they have to charge you with, be sure it caused no injury to anyone whatsoever.

William Calhoun, you bore your misery with fortitude. Many of us were aware that your first entrance into the work world was a bumpy move. You looked like a professional golfer driving that log truck. You were not one who formed an elevated view of those who ran our community or, for that matter, our culture. Still, you proceeded in your career into better jobs. As you increased in affluence you did not rise above the fray and conflict and merge with those you despised. I never heard you complain of any misfortune. I never noticed any disturbance on your part at the level of contempt which ill fortune had dealt to you earlier. In fact, your spirit never urged you to solicit reconciliation. You returned reproach for reproach and insult for insult. Your wit enabled you to move beyond and make jokes about it. Your presence was sufficient to draw many people, and your example constituted fashion in some circles. Your personality was so powerful that others were pleased to have the opportunity of gratifying their vanity by hanging out with you. I was one of those people.

Like many of us, maybe you continued to act upon the same principles and follow the same path in life. Maybe you were never made wiser by your suffering. In some ways you proceeded through your short life to tread steps on the same circle, turning your eyes from the light of reason which would have illuminated the illusion and shown you the real state of our broken world. But my friend, no apology or regrets are necessary. If you failed, then so do we; if your work appears to be unfinished, then so does ours. No one exists or has ever existed on this earth who can judge your conduct and no wise man or woman can say had I been in William Calhoun Fisher's situation I could have done better. Rest in peace my brother ... you are much loved.

Rest in Peace Mayor

The seasons were changing and the heat and humidity seemed much less oppressive. Fall storms were beginning to blow. Earlier in the spring the mayor was defeated in the Vicksburg mayoral race. He had served for three terms and done a most excellent job; industry had come in and the economy was thriving. The city had a new Westinghouse Plant and the Harbor Project on the river had other businesses lining up to locate there. A local used car salesman with no political experience defeated him; the defeat was unexplainable. Because of his age, the mayor's political career was over and he was devastated. In his depression and loss he became seriously ill. He went to the Sisters of Mercy Hospital in Vicksburg and was stunned to receive a terminal diagnosis. Going home, he just sat and suffered for days, not knowing what to do. Several of his friends visited him and tried to give comfort with no positive result until his longtime friend Jim, an attorney in town, suggested that he get a second opinion. The mayor was interested and he immediately set up an appointment at Ochsner Hospital in New Orleans. Jim agreed to drive the mayor and two of his closest buddies, Izadore Fader and Jimmy Laughlin, down to New Orleans for the appointment.

Jimmy was known as Bear. Bear arrived at Jim's

house at 7 a.m. and parked his car. They left immediately to pick up the mayor at his home just off Washington Street, then they drove to get gas at Waring's service station. Word had spread all over town regarding the mayor's illness and Daniel Pearson Waring, the station owner, left his breakfast uneaten and walked across the street from the Hotel Vicksburg coffee shop to wish the former mayor good luck. After the fill-up, they stopped for Izadore, known as Izzy, at his elaborate home on Signal Hill south of town, the highest point between Memphis and New Orleans.

Coming out of his home, Izzy let out a low whistle when he saw Jim's vehicle. "Jim, where did you get the T-Bird?"

"We got it at Dalrymple Ford last week. Pauline wanted it. It's really more than we needed."

Izzy laughed, made a facial gesture, and said, "It sure beats that old Country Squire Pauline had. What happened to it?"

Jim started down the drive and said, "Last week I got home late. Pauline had asked me to stop at Klein's and get supper for the kids. I forgot and the kids and I got back in the car and were backing out of the driveway. My daughter forgot to close the door and I ripped it backward on the hedges."

The men laughed heartily as Jim continued down Izzy's long driveway and proceeded south on Highway 61. They could not help but notice massive storm clouds to the north. The group settled in and adjusted their ties and tried to get comfortable. Izzy had his briefcase at his feet and Bear asked if he had brought anything to drink. Izzy nodded, reached in his briefcase and passed a fifth of Early Times over to Bear who opened it, took a long pull and commented, "Man, look at those dark clouds up north. I hope we don't get that storm on the way."

"Bear, maybe tomorrow but not today," Jim replied. "The storm is moving south at a slow pace according to the weather reports."

Everyone was silent for several miles as they looked at the passing scenery coming to life. At one point north of Port Gibson a number of deer emerged from the forest and started toward the highway. Jim slowed down as the deer began to cross the road. Then a massive buck emerged and bolted across the road and disappeared into the woods behind the does. Taking another pull of whiskey, Bear muttered, "Wish I had my shotgun; we'd have enough meat for months." Picking up speed again, Jim continued down the road. The landscape became a sea of pine trees that Anderson Tully Lumber Company had planted on farm land purchased to supply lumber products. They went through Port Gibson and passed the famous church with a hand on the steeple top pointing upwards towards the sky. Jim poured a cup of coffee from a thermos and offered a cup to the others but no one was ready yet. They continued in silence and contemplation with regard to what the mayor faced.

North of Fayette, Izzy stretched and rubbed his hands over the opulent car seat and said, "Man this vehicle is smooth, Jim. It out rates that old Model A you had in high school, the one you took on that trip out west your senior year. You had asked me to go but I couldn't. Remind me Jim, who wound up going with you?"

Laughing, Jim replied, "Jim Cunningham and Red Jacobson came. I've never forgotten Red's comment when he was feeding a bear in Yellowstone and we were taking pictures of him. Something jammed on the little Brownie camera my sister had loaned me and we signaled Red to jerk the food away until we could get the camera fixed. The bear smacked and clawed Red and chased him up on top of the Model A. Red regained his composure and said, 'I don't know about y'all but I ain't sleeping here tonight.'" Spilling his whiskey, Bear laughed uproariously. Izzy likewise laughed but the mayor did not even crack a smile.

Approaching the town of Lorman, Izzy asked Jim if he would stop at Cohn Brothers General Store so he could speak to the owners, Hyman and his wife Jane. Jim stopped and Izzy went into the store. The clerk informed him that the Cohns were on a month long river cruise on the Delta Queen. Getting back into the car, Izzy said, "Won't see them this trip; they are cruising the Mississippi River."

Getting back on the highway, Jim said, "I would have liked to see Hyman and Jane again. They are nice folks."

After another taste of whiskey, Bear said, "Jim your speech at the Veterans of Foreign Wars meeting last night was marvelous. I loved it when you pulled your new baby's booty out when you were reaching for your speech. Was that an accident or a planned incident?" Everybody excluding the mayor laughed again.

Smiling, Jim answered, "Oh, I thought that they would be more accepting if they knew that I had a new child. I used the same trick ten years ago when I was running for the state senate and it worked." Turning around to the mayor, Jim asked, "How are you feeling Mayor?"

The mayor opened his eyes and replied, "I feel a little rough but I'll make it." Upon hearing the comment everyone turned and looked at the mayor.

Izzy said, "Mayor, I'm feeling rough too. I just opened my new store at Eagle Lake called Fin & Feathers and I was up there until 3 a.m. with a big rowdy crowd."

Putting the cap back on the bottle, Bear chimed in, "Izzy, I heard about your new place. Are you going to keep your store on Levee Street? I love that sign down there 'tell em where you got it....' By the way I never understood how you sold liquor down there with our state being dry."

Izzy looked quizzically at Bear. "Of course I'm going to keep the Levee Street store open. We sold booze under a policy called local option. Our community decided that they need booze and I'm here to provide it for them, Bear." Again the T-Bird resonated with laughter.

The mayor reminisced as he looked out the window. "Every time I have driven down this road to New Orleans it felt like I was going back in time. My wife and I used to come down once a year and it felt like we were driving into the mid-eighteen hundreds as we passed through Port Gibson, Fayette, and Natchez. I love this area."

Izzy placed his hand on the mayor's shoulder and commented, "I agree Mayor. I needed to get out of town. I needed a break and what better place to be with you than in this historical area."

Bear loosened his tie even more and the others did the same and shifted in the bucket seats. Bear asked, "Where are we staying down in New Orleans?"

Jim replied, "The Fontainebleau on Tulane Avenue."

The mayor turned his head from the window and asked, "Do y'all remember the Sugar Bowl when Ole Miss beat LSU 21-zip? My wife and I were there; it was just before my wife died, bless her heart. It was the best trip I've ever had to New Orleans, better than this one will be I'm sure. We stayed at the Fontainebleau. The Ole Miss team was there and Coach Vaught did not let them get out at night and roam; the team was most disciplined that weekend." After a brief pause, the mayor added, "Speaking of Ole Miss, Jim, didn't you play up there when I was a senior?"

Shaking his head, Jim responded, "Mayor all I did was try out; I did not belong out there. I was just trying to impress the girls. In my last practice, we were drilling and Bully White knocked me out cold." Again laughter filled the moving car.

The mayor replied, "I remember Bully, he was an All-American, wasn't he?"

Jim nodded and replied. "Yes he was. And it hurt when he hit you. I was lying on the field and I woke up in time to hear our freshman coach, Tadpole Smith, say somebody drag Rosenbloom off the field. Obviously Tadpole could not pronounce or remember my name."

Izzy laughed, "He must have thought you were Jewish, with your long name it wouldn't be too hard to do."

Bear and Izzy chuckled. Jim snarled, "Yeah, well whatever, Tadpole and I didn't speak for years after that and I was finished with football for good." Changing the subject, Jim continued. "I need a break, I know most of you have not had any breakfast. We can eat in Natchez. Anybody have any ideas?"

The mayor spoke up first. "I'd like to eat at Conley's Tavern. The food is excellent. My old girlfriend owns it and she wanted to see me before my appointment at Ochsner." Neither Izzy nor Bear voiced any objection.

Continuing the journey, they worked their way south through Fayette toward Natchez. The countryside was verdant and farmers were out on tractors harvesting corn, cotton, and soybeans. The sun was high and the sky to the south was clear. Rounding a curve, Jim saw a long line of cars backed up. Down the highway he could see a log truck rolled over on its side blocking the road; its massive load had tumbled out and was scattered along the road. Several highway patrol vehicles and two ambulances were on the scene with lights flashing. Tow trucks waited to move the overturned vehicle. Jim muttered, "Maybe it won't take too long to get past this wreck. I hope nobody was hurt." Within fifteen minutes, the two ambulances screeched north toward Vicksburg transporting the injured. It took the tow trucks another hour to clear the road before the line of cars on both sides began to start moving. Finally passing the wreck, the men were shocked to see that the log truck had landed on a pick-up truck and crushed it. Blood was all over the road and several folks stood crying on the shoulder of the highway.

As they moved past the wreckage, Bear exclaimed, "Look! That smashed pickup has Warren County tags. Anybody recognize it? I hope it's not anybody we know because whoever it was did not survive."

Izzy commented, "It looks like Dan Coles truck to me but why would he be down this way?"

Looking at the overturned truck, the mayor noticed a highway patrolman he recognized. He lowered the window and called to the patrolman, "Officer Terrill, who was in the pickup?"

The officer said, "Mayor, don't know for sure. There were three men in the cab. Two of them are injured severely and are on the way to the hospital in Vicksburg. The driver is still in the truck. Looks like we'll have to cut him out. The two guys in the log truck survived and are Likewise on the way to the hospital."

Rolling his window up, the mayor replied, "Thanks officer!"

An hour later the group pulled into Natchez. Arriving at Conley's Tavern, the men walked in under an old sign with faded letters stating that the tavern was founded in 1844. The group was escorted to their table and given menus. The tavern was cozy and well decorated: linen table cloths and napkins, silver utensils; the furniture was antique and beautiful and each table had candles in antique holders which the waitress lit once the group sat down. While looking over the menu, Izzy said "Well it's too late for breakfast but man I'm hungry; I hope the food hasn't been here since 1844 whoa!"

Returning from the restroom, Bear said, "I'm

hungry too. Mayor, are you nervous about meeting your old love? I know that I would be if I had one."

Still looking over the menu, Izzy said, "Bear, I thought that you were married recently to that Taylor woman with the three kids."

Picking up his menu, Bear replied, "Nah Izzy, she left me months ago."

The men kicked back in their seats near the window and surveyed the menu. Moments later Jim whispered, "Mayor, here she comes." The men turned around and saw a beautiful woman walking towards their table. The mayor slowly looked up and saw his old love walking towards him with a concerned look on her face. She gave the Mayor a long hug. Overcome, the mayor kissed her on the cheek and promptly introduced Laura Lee to his companions.

After meeting everyone. Laura Lee asked, "Jim, aren't you an attorney? I think I was on a jury one time when you tried a case in Natchez. It was a long time ago."

Jim smiled at her, "Well thank you for remembering. Did we win?"

Laura Lee smiled, "No. Your defendant was convicted and sentenced to be executed. Frowning, Izzy looked out the window and rolled his eyes. Laura Lee asked,

"Pat, can you come to my office for a moment. I have something to give you."

Getting up, the mayor said, "Jim, order a shrimp po-boy for me please."

Once inside the office Laura Lee closed the door and handed him an envelope. Holding the mayor's hand, she said, "Pat, I had a child by you over twenty years ago and never told you. She lives in New Orleans now and never knew who her father was. I want you to take this to her and introduce yourself. The letter says that you are the former mayor of Vicksburg and that you are her dad. I believe it will mean a lot to her. I also tell her in the letter that you are a wonderful man and we just were not meant to be together. And I told her that you are very ill."

The mayor choked and stammered. "Why didn't you tell me? Where does she live? How can I find her?"

"She owns the PhD Pole Bar at the end of Bourbon Street. She also performs in the club. She was married for several years to a pro-golfer and had a normal life going, but her hubby turned out to be a bad boy and things did not work."

The mayor stumbled to a chair and sat down. "Laura Lee, why didn't you tell me?"

"I just couldn't. I loved you very much, but there was no way you and I could have made it." As the mayor slumped in his seat, Laura Lee offered, "Let me get you a glass of water and help you relax."

Back at the table, the men the waitress returned. Jim said, "What do y'all want to eat?"

Bear said, "I trust the mayor, let's have the po-boy."

Izzy took a sip of his water and said, "Good enough for me. I haven't eaten since lunch yesterday."

The waitress wrote the orders down for four shrimp po-boys and asked,

"How about drinks?" Bear ordered beer and Jim and Izzy ordered coffee for themselves and the mayor.

Stretching, Izzy asked, "Jim, have you tried many cases down in Natchez?

"Not really. My partner and I worked with a lawyer down here on several cases when we were just getting started. I remember the case to which Laura Lee referred. The gentleman was subsequently executed. It was first electric chair execution in Mississippi. Let me assure you that our firm really paid dearly for it when pictures appeared in newspapers all over the state of my partner and I witnessing our client being electrocuted."

The dining room was loud with customer's conversations when Bear asked, "Jim, did you know Charlie Champion down here?"

Jim finished a bite of food and replied, "I roomed with him my freshman year in law school. Nice guy. Haven't seen him in years."

Likewise swallowing a bite of his sandwich, Bear said, "I don't know him but my cousin told me that he was shot outside the courtroom during a volatile case and is incapacitated now."

Shocked, Jim uttered, "What? When?"

"Maybe 3 months ago."

Jim muttered, "Oh my Lord. I had no idea."

Izzy joined the conversation. "Another lawyer was

shot and killed recently outside the Port Gibson court-house."

Jim replied, "Now, that shooting I knew about. It was Lamar Johnson. Things are coming unraveled."

The men were almost finished before the mayor returned from his meeting. He clutched the letter in his hand. He sat silently. Izzy questioned, "What's wrong Mayor?"

Bear added a codicil, "Buck up Mayor, yo shrimp awaits."

The mayor put his hands over his face. "Laura Lee just told me that she had a child by me years ago. Patricia is her name and she is in her mid-twenties and lives in New Orleans. She is a striptease dancer and club owner. Laura Lee gave me this letter to take her. I am stunned and mortified; I have no idea what to do."

Moved with compassion, Jim said, "Well mayor, it is your decision but if you want we can take her the letter after supper tonight. Where is her club?"

The mayor tearfully replied, "It's down on Bourbon; it's called The PhD Pole club.

Sipping his third beer, Bear said, "That's an odd name for a strip club. What's the point?"

Regaining his composure, the mayor replied, "Laura Lee told me that the strippers dress in motor boards and graduation gowns which they remove during their act. It attracts many college professors and students."

Picking up the bill, Jim asked, "What do you want to do Mayor?"

The mayor pushed his plate away and said, "I must meet her and tell her I am her father; she never knew who her dad was. I'm very sick; I can't delay this. It may be my last chance to atone."

The rest of the trip to the Crescent City was quiet. Jim drove, Bear sipped Early Times, Izzy looked out the window thinking, and the mayor napped restlessly in his seat.

The men arrived in New Orleans late in the late afternoon. After checking in at the Fontainebleau Hotel, they decided to eat at TuJacques and go to the PhD Pole Club after dinner. At dinner, the mayor was quiet. Jim watched him compassionately. Izzy was contemplative and Bear was inebriated and talkative. When they finished eating, the men walked over to nearby Bourbon Street. Bear was excited and looking forward to the strip show. Entering the club, the Mayor immediately sought out the matre de and told him that he had an urgent note for Miss Patricia. The matre de escorted the Mayor to the back area of the club. He left him on a large bumpy couch just outside the dressing room and told him that Miss Patricia would be out shortly. The other men were escorted to a table near the stage and took their seats.

The club was packed; every table was occupied. The lighting and curtains on the stage and in the show room were very elaborate. A comedian gave his performance as the strippers waited in the wings. Most customers were looking at the stripers who peeked from behind the curtain and not paying any attention to the comedian who was not very funny. Bored with the comedian, Izzy commented, "Jim this guy is terrible. Let me ask you something before the gals come on stage. I can't completely remember your VFW speech last night, but didn't you say that you were arrested in Berlin just before we entered the war? What was that about?"

Jim sighed. "I had just graduated from law school and took a trip to Europe before I started my law practice. I was in a Berlin bar one night in between the invasion of Austria and Poland and the clientele was singing praises to Adolph Hitler. I finally got tired of it and said something to the guy next to me at the bar. He was a Nazi agent of some sort and he had me arrested. I was in jail all that night and would probably have never been seen again if Germany had not been worried about the United States entering the war. They let me go the next morning provided I agreed to leave Germany immediately."

Izzy reflected on what could have happened to Jim and asked, "Didn't you volunteer for the Army after that?"

"Yes, I saw what was coming. I joined the year before Pearl Harbor and was sent to the Pacific just after the Japanese attacked us."

"Weren't you in the field artillery?"

"I was."

Izzy continued, "Jim, I joined a year or more after

you and served in Europe but I remember a story going around Vicksburg before I left. I think you sent it to your parents in a letter. You were looking for artillery quadrants and you pulled up to a foxhole on Luzon and got out of your jeep with your binocs and asked the soldier in the foxhole where the front line was. He peaked out from under his helmet and replied, 'I was, now you is.' Somebody said that you told him to move over."

The crowd clapped loudly as the comedian finished and Bear, who was eagerly awaiting the strippers, said, "Jim, what you said about Luzon was funnier than anything that man said up there." The band in the corner cranked up and the girls came on stage amid much clapping and cheering. The goal of these dancers was to warm up the crowd for Patricia's performance. Everyone in the audience focused on the attractive dancers who moved all over the stage dipping and strutting. Jim, Izzy, and Bear could not resist watching the beautiful, attractive young ladies as they entertained the crowd.

In the dressing area, the Mayor rose as his daughter approached him wearing the graduation gown and mortar board. Patricia walked over to the couch and said, "The matre de said that you have an urgent note for me. What can I do for you sir? I don't have much time."

The mayor replied, "Patricia, I have a note from your mother." He handed it to her; she ripped it open and read it and stumbled back stunned and shocked. The mayor continued. "I just found out today that I am your father." Patricia replied, "Sir, I have to process this information. I will have to contact my mom and confirm this." Moving towards the show room and wiping a tear from her eye, Patricia said, "I have to go on stage now. I will call Mom after my show and see if she confirms this."

He nodded sadly and watched her walk away with the black gown flowing and the motor board crooked on her head. "I'm staying at the Fontainebleau with some friends. I am down here for an appointment at Ochsner tomorrow morning." He couldn't tell whether she heard him or not but he joined his friends at the table for Patricia's entre.

The band cranked up again as Patricia emerged and

went on stage. The other girls stepped into their routine and whirled gracefully as Patricia joined them. The audience was calling loudly and intensely for the robes to come off. Off they came, beginning with one girl who removed her graduation robe and flung her motor board to the ceiling. Each dancer followed suit until the only one robed was Patricia. Knowing what was about to happen the Mayor covered his eyes, but Bear could not look away. What he witnessed was most exciting. Patricia removed her robe and was truly beautiful. A pole descended from the ceiling and Patricia performed a pole dance while the others danced behind her.

When the performance ended and the curtain dropped, Izzy said, "Well I see why this place is so busy." They stood and prepared to leave with the exception of Bear who wanted more and the mayor who sat sadly in his seat with his eyes covered.

Patricia called the Fontainebleau Hotel early in the morning and told the mayor that her mom had confirmed the letter and that she was willing to meet for breakfast after his appointment. She gave him her street address on Rampart and said that she would be waiting. After checking out of the Fontainebleau, the men drove to Ochsner hospital where the mayor received the worst of news. Basically the doctor told the mayor to go home, press his suit and find a casket because there was nothing they could do.

Back in the Thunder Bird, the men were silent as they drove to the French Quarter. None of them knew what to say. Turning down Rampart Street to Patricia's home, they picked her up and proceeded to Brennan's for breakfast. Conversation at the meal was trite and uncomfortable. The other men said very little and did their best to let their friend and his daughter talk. The mayor and Patricia spoke quietly about his terminal diagnosis. After the meal, they returned the mayor's daughter to her home. Patricia leaned over and gave the mayor a kiss on his cheek as she exited the vehicle and slipped him her phone number. He watched sadly as she disappeared in the rear window when the T-Bird pulled off leaving her on the curb watching.

Leaving town, there was little conversation. Jim turned north on Highway 61 and once out of town conversation picked up again. Jim began. "Mayor, I know that you are upset about the bad news but many doctors don't include the divine in their diagnosis these days. You can just pray for a miracle."

The mayor replied softly, "Jim I am not worried about getting well. It is over for me. I have fallen short. I need forgiveness, mercy and grace. Look at the mess I have made. My little girl is a stripper."

Kindly, Jim replied, "We all stray Mayor. You have been an honest politician and a good man. You are much loved in Vicksburg. You are no worse than any of us and Patricia seemed to be a nice young lady in spite of her occupation."

The mayor wiped away tears and said, "Seeing my daughter last night as she stripped was so painful. If I had known maybe I could have helped her have a normal life. Her mom told me that Patricia was a normal housewife for a while and married to a pro golfer, but it did not work out at all and she went into this business." He dropped his head and sobbed as the others looked away.

After the mayor regained his composure, Jim said, "Mayor, I realize that you were wounded by your loss in the election this spring and now these situations you are facing are most difficult. But we all fall far short. Look around you; look in this car. You are surrounded by broken sinners. But God forgives us should we seek it."

Still tearful, the Mayor responded, "I know. I've gone to church all my life. I've heard the words, but I never turned to the Lord on a deeper level. I never really sought him. So I have not attained that blessing and probably never will now."

Trying to encourage the mayor, Jim said, "Mayor, there is a difference between words and knowing. But the struggle is between thinking we know and living the truth. Hearing is not enough. We all hear the words but it is most important to seek. Recently during the times of trouble our church had armed guards outside the sanctuary blocking certain people from coming in. I stood up in a meeting and said let them in. They won't stay. They will be bored to tears. They voted to keep the guards in place.

Then we discussed spending thousands on a new sanctuary rug. I suggested putting a poor kid through college with the money; they opted for the rug. I knew then that the message of the Gospel was distorted and spiritual life was reduced to a false proposition. I never went back. That was all she wrote for me. But the heart of God's teaching tells us that we can be transformed in spite of the state of this broken world and our mistakes. All we have to do is believe in him and then seek the deeper relationship that is offered. The truth is that most of us in some ways fall far short of that lesson but God extends his grace and mercy and we should Likewise forgive ourselves."

Joining the conversation, Izzy said, "Mayor, like Jim I fall short too. We all sin, we all do; we need the forgiveness offered by God's unconditional love and we miss the mark. We refuse God's forgiveness and remain bound by neurotic guilt. It is up to us to accept what God offers and it is not as hard as people think. It is as simple as the words in those old hymns like 'Jesus loves me this I know' or 'On Christ the solid rock I stand all other ground is shifting sand.' Listen Mayor, like Jim I don't go to church but all of us can energetically grasp for God's grace and mercy. Forgiveness is a gift freely given; it brings wholeness not perfection. It brings completion and maturity. So Mayor, the door is wide open for you and all of us. Confession of our sin involves a change in our relationship with God and a change within us. Only then we can reach reconciliation with our creator."

At this Bear took another pull of Early Times and muttered, "I hope he forgives me." Izzy snatched the bottle away from Bear and put the top back on it.

Jim said, "Mayor, every adult I know in Vicksburg drinks, but for me drinking was a big part of hiding my scars from the war. When I stopped drinking, I got much closer to the Lord and began the process of transformation of which the Lord spoke. I thought not drinking was simply not drinking but it brought a bigger opportunity for me and my relationship with God."

Izzy added, "Mayor, like I said ... I don't even attend church but I love to read stuff about faith. Recently I was reading a *Saturday Evening Post* article on how the physical and the spiritual are becoming separated in our culture.

Forgiveness today is reduced to something that is unnecessary and healing is suspect because it is outside the scientific framework. Our culture separates the spiritual and the physical, and such thinking affects our relationship with God and has a profound effect on our health and wellbeing. We are seen as passive spectators of our illness. We are not encouraged to become actively engaged in the process of seeking forgiveness and healing." Bear reached for the Early Times but Izzy waved him off and continued. "Mayor, when I did attend church, I got sick of the constant chatter about a heavenly friend with gentle lessons about the truth constantly telling us that we can receive anything we long for or desire. Even I understand that it is bigger than that. Like all of us, you have an opening before you, but you are angry at yourself and that anger blocks God's help."

Jim looked at the mayor and said, "What Izzy is telling you is that it is easy to get trapped in our anger. Holding on to anger delays the movement toward forgiveness and letting go. The only way to correct this pattern is to unlock the pain and anger and release them to God."

Izzy continued. "That same *Saturday Evening Post* article that I recently read said that most people in our culture live their entire existence in a box. In this box we deny any reality which cannot be rationally qualified or measured. Even committed folks of faith have difficulty believing that any reality exists outside this box of which we speak. But we are badly mistaken. The spiritual world encompasses the physical world and gives it meaning."

The car became quiet for a period as everybody except Bear thought about what had been said. At Tickfaw the sky opened up; the storm that they had noticed up north yesterday had moved south with a vengeance. Jim switched on the wipers and lights and slowed down. No one spoke as they maneuvered through the terrible weather. After they crossed the state line, the storm let up slightly. Shifting in his seat, the mayor said, "Well fellows, I realize that I have spent my life in that box to which Izzy referred. I am near the end. I have messed up."

"But Mayor," Jim exclaimed, "all this is the work of the Holy Spirit, not a struggle of your will. Your hope is to seek God's forgiveness and then forgive yourself."

Sadly the mayor replied, "In my lifetime, I wore a mask which seemed to be real and I ignored the hidden inner person who God created. My ego self was who and what the world told me I was. I protected this false self with rigid patterns of behavior in my life and in my career."

Jim shook his head sadly and exchanged glances with Izzy, who then made his final comment to the mayor. "Mayor, none of this truth comes to us like knowledge or logic; it is not rational, but it yields a light that transforms our nature. The best response for us is to utter 'God is my life; it is not I who live but God who lives in me.'"

Closing the conversation, the mayor said, "Boys, maybe even if I die God will shed his grace on me. In the Bible Psalm 63 tells us that he ardently seeks us in death as well as life."

They drove on in silence for an hour. When they reached Lorman again, the storm had passed. They stopped again at Cohn's General Store. Everybody got out to urinate except the mayor. Bear got out of the car almost before it stopped and staggered ahead while Jim and Izzy avoided the numerous puddles while walking toward the store. Bear rushed directly to the restroom but Jim and Izzy stopped at the desk and asked the clerk if he knew who was hurt or killed in the logging truck wreck yesterday. Already finished in the restroom, Bear exited the store as the clerk answered that the driver of the log truck survived with injuries and the driver of the pickup truck was killed but a man riding in the log truck and two others in the pickup suffered relatively minor injuries and are still in the hospital in Vicksburg. Izzy asked, "Do you know who was driving the pickup?" The clerk replied that it was a man from Vicksburg named Dan Cole. Jim and Izzy shook their heads sadly and continued toward the restroom.

In the restroom, Izzy said, "Jim, I don't think we reached Mayor at all."

"No we didn't, but we tried."

"What happens now? I don't think that the *Saturday Evening Post* can tell me."

Jim smiled. "Don't worry Izzy. The mayor is like most people on earth. He is a good man who did not go quite far enough spiritually. I'm not judging at all. This malady has been most common throughout history. Even today only 15% of believers seek a deeper relationship with the Lord. But mercy and forgiveness are promised to believers, even you and me and Bear. Think of it this way: We're all on the same road, and some are further along than others. But no matter where you are on the journey, God still loves you; it is not a race or a contest. Even Bear is loved. Don't worry. The mayor will be blessed in spite of his flaws and shortcomings. We all will."

Bear stumbled and staggered through the mud puddles to the car. He found his honor the mayor slumped on the seat dead and gone. Bear reached in the car and retrieved the bottle, took a long pull, and said, "Rest in peace Mayor."

Harvard's Only Bubba

C.H. was a lieutenant colonel; his wife Francis was the sibling of Mary, Herman, Warner and my dad James. C. H. and Francis had two children. Donnie was adopted in New Orleans and Bubba was born in Vicksburg. Uncle C.H. had served in the European Theatre during World War II. Afterwards he continued to serve in the army, and he and his family lived in Japan; Brooklyn, New York; Norfolk, Virginia; and Germany.

Aunt Francis came home to Vicksburg as often as possible with Donnie and Bubba to visit the family. They would stay at her mom's home on Markham Street and visitors would flock to the house. Warner Jr. was Bubba's age; Donnie was older and Herman and I were five or six years younger. Our younger brothers, David and Richard, were ten years younger than Herman and I. All of us looked forward to their visits. The first visit I remember was at Christmas time. When Aunt Francis pulled up in front of grandmother's house on Markham Street, Bubba and Donnie jumped out of the vehicle and ran up the steep hill to the house where we greeted them cordially.

The next day we toured the Vicksburg Military Park with Uncle Herman, who was also home for Christmas. We met at grandmother's house and crawled into Uncle Herman's Buick and drove all over the battlefield. Warner and Bubba were in the front seat with Uncle Herman; Donnie, Herman and I were in the back; David and Richard were too young then to tour with us. It was chilly but the day was beautiful and sunny. Uncle Herman knew that the park rangers had a program planned for that morning at the redoubt where General Logan's Illinois forces attacked the Confederates on Graveyard Road. We all exited the car and listened to the lecture. Bubba intently took notes on the bloody conflict.

After the park ranger's program, we drove around stopping at various monuments. Donnie would run over and climb onto the statue and ask us to take his picture. Uncle Herman would sigh and send Bubba over to retrieve Donnie. We went to the cemetery below Fort Nogales, which was filled with Union soldiers, and parked under a tree; Uncle Herman asked us where we would like to go next. We all screamed Fort Nogales, so Uncle Herman started up the hill to the fort. When we crossed Mint Springs, Donnie asked Uncle Herman to stop, and then he jumped out of the car and stood on the bridge rail asking Bubba to photograph him. Bubba shook his head, got out of the Buick and started toward the rail just as Donnie slipped into the cold creek. Donnie emerged shivering and Uncle Herman got a blanket out of the trunk and handed it to him.

We continued to the fort and Donnie stayed in the car as the rest of us went up the side of Fort Nogales and looked deep into Louisiana across the Mississippi River. When we returned to the car we drove into town and stopped at the Magnolia Dairy, which Warner, Herman and David's dad, owned and managed. Bubba got a large vanilla shake; Donnie came out of his blanket and ordered an even larger double banana split. Warner, Herman and I settled for single cones. The next day we rode up to Long Lake with Uncle Herman and fished off the dock; nobody caught any fish but it was fun. Several days later Aunt Francis and her sons were on the way back to Japan and Uncle Herman was back in San Antonio, Texas.

The next visit was summer time. The adults were all in the living room visiting with Grandmother. Warner, Herman and I were looking for Donnie and Bubba in hopes that one of the adults would take us up to the Redwood swimming hole north of town. We could hear Bubba's heavy footsteps in the breakfast nook so we sent our younger brothers back there to find them. They returned with no results. Warner, Herman, and I then went and searched. Herman was standing next to the breakfast nook seats when we heard Donnie fussing at his brother to stop kicking him. As we opened the seat top, we all jumped back startled; Bubba and Donnie were curled up in the interior of the nook seats smiling up at us wearing German helmets that Uncle Warner had brought home after WWII. It was so crowded in there that we had to help them get up and out of their hiding spot.

On another trip Aunt Francis and her sons arrived after the long trip from Germany. Grandmother had passed away and Aunt Mary now resided in the family home on Markham Street. The next day Aunt Francis and Aunt Jo Willa took all of us—Bubba, Donnie, Warner, Herman, David, Richard, and me—to the Sisters of Mercy Convent to visit Sister Clementine, our great aunt. All of us except Bubba and Donnie were protestant so we called her Aunt Annie; she was our grandmother's sister. The visit went wonderfully well. Aunt Annie met us in a room at the convent. We all were most fond of Sister Clementine and she brought out treats for us to consume while we visited.

After the convent visit we went to the city pool and had a swim. We were frolicking and playing in the sun. I remember being shocked at how large Bubba was in his swimming suit. I was swimming with Herman under the high diving board when Bubba jumped off. He landed directly on Herman and I and we both sank quickly to the bottom of the pool. Bubba surfaced laughing and Herman and I surfaced coughing and wheezing. Aunt Jo Willa was greatly relieved that no one was hurt. Then we went to Johnny's restaurant for lunch.

We went to the Miss-Lou Fair the next day. I remember the crowds and the rides and the cotton candy. We were all having a good time; we rode the Ferris wheel, the roller coaster and whatever was available. Then we saw the bumper cars; all of us excitedly lined up and took a car. We sped around the arena spinning and whirling. Then

Bubba's car took a curve and spun around and hit me head on. I will never forget the massive jar I felt when we collided. I think what made the impact so pounding was the fact that Bubba was so much larger than I was at the time. From that point on I avoided his vehicle as much as possible.

We enjoyed these trips immensely and looked forward to them. But everything changed. Uncle Herman started bringing his girlfriend Thelma and her son Jackie when he came home for Christmas. Back in Germany, Donnie was already in high school and it was more difficult for Francis to arrange trips home. Bubba's academic career began in earnest when he started high school two years after Donnie. He had excellent grades and was most athletic, becoming the wrestling champ of American military schools in Germany. After graduating high school, Donnie joined the army. In Bubba's senior year, he applied for West Point. We were all hopeful that he would be accepted but he could not lift his massive frame up on the chin-up bar enough times, so he was rejected. He then applied to Harvard University.

After Bubba graduated from high school and was accepted at Harvard, C.H. retired from the army and he and Francis moved back to Vicksburg. Donnie had likewise finished his army tenure and returned home a few months before his parents. He was living at the YMCA and roaming all over town in his used Chevy convertible, and he started dating a massive girl named Pat. One night Herman, Warner, and I were visiting with Donnie and Pat. My tongue slipped and I accidentally called her fat instead of Pat. I thought she was ready to flip the table and come after me. Warner and Herman were roaring with laughter; Donnie had lowered his head and covered his eyes. I felt bad about my mistake and apologized quickly and she calmed down.

After that first year at Harvard, Bubba came to spend the summer in Vicksburg. He worked for the Coca Cola plant, which was owned and managed by one of our relatives, Trappy, who was married to Jo Willa's sister Ruth. While preparing to return to Harvard after his summer in Vicksburg, Bubba borrowed a confederate uniform from a Civil War re-enactor and told us of his plans to do a skit on Stonewall Jackson's birthday. We blew it off as a bad idea but to the contrary it became most popular at Harvard. Many students were heartily entertained and interested and took the trouble to attend.

The summer after his junior year Bubba came home and was caught up in the time of trouble and racial turmoil our community was facing. He was back at the Coke plant working and several of the drivers resented his Harvard tee shirts and his openness towards others. One day two Coke drivers jumped Bubba and beat him into submission; Bubba was athletic and strong but boxing was not his game. He was battered and bloody but he did not cave. Soon after Bubba's beating, Donnie was chased with his new girlfriend out of Schuler's Waltz Inn on the edge of the Delta north of town. They jumped into Donny's old Chevy convertible and sped down highway 61 and up Clay Street as the troublemakers followed them with tire thumpers and baseball bats. We thought that maybe they knew that Donny was Bubba's brother and they attacked him for that reason, but no one ever knew why the attack occurred. Oddly Donny was the only one arrested; my dad put a young lawyer in his firm on the case and Donnie was exonerated.

Bubba was troubled by the conflict that he and Donnie had faced and he began interesting and deep discussions with my father that summer at our house. I sat silent and mesmerized as they talked. Dad's law firm was defending James Silver, the author of *Mississippi: The Closed Society* and Dad had been threatened many times and understood what Bubba was going through. After the talks Bubba would jog back to his parent's home on Drummond Street. My father instructed me to follow Bubba from a distance in our family car. I never really understood what I would do if trouble occurred.

The last time I ever had with Bubba was when we went to a drive-in movie to see *Of Human Bondage* starring Lawrence Harvey. It was the night before Bubba left for his senior year at Harvard. At the drive-in, we talked the whole time about family and politics. I was upset about the turmoil in our community and Bubba was very understanding of my perspective. I was most pleased to have had such a conversation with him. I admired him very

much. Bubba left the next morning in his recently purchased used VW. The final year at Harvard went well; he
performed his last skit and was successful academically,
graduating Magna Cum Laude. His life was before him; he
had plans and dreams.

We got the sad news late in the afternoon. Bubba had
crashed his car and died on the way home from Harvard.
He had recently been diagnosed with Diabetes and had
lost consciousness. He swerved off the highway and hit
a tree. Our family of cousins, uncles, and aunts began to
gather sadly at Bubba's parents' home. His brother Donnie
was standing on the front porch with Warner Jr. when my
family and I arrived. Donnie was weeping and uttering, "It
should have been me."
    C.H. was employed at the Waterways Experiment
Station in Vicksburg and many of his colleagues were
there in addition to our kinfolk. Richard and David went
to the toy box which Aunt Francis kept for them. Warner,
Herman, and I began to wander around the house; we met
C.H. standing in the hall near the telephone. C.H. was devastated and tearful and he was muttering something about
Clancy. Herman and I exchanged glances trying to figure
out who Clancy could be. After C.H. wandered down
the hall to Bubba's room, Warner told us that Clancy was
Bubba's nickname when he lived in Germany. Herman and
I had never known that.
    Warner, Herman, and I walked into the kitchen
where Francis sat quietly at the table, weeping. She was
surrounded by Aunt Mary, Aunt Jo Willa, and Aunt Pauline. Francis acknowledged our presence; we hugged her
and tiptoed back to the living room. C.H.'s colleagues from
work had begun to leave and we sat with family. After
an hour or two, Warner Sr. and my dad went to Goldie's
BBQ to fetch some supper for Francis, C.H., and Donnie.
We sat with Francis and C.H. as they picked at the food
numbly.
    The priest from St. Paul's arrived soon afterwards.
He let C.H. and Francis know that he had just met with
the funeral director; Bubba's body would be flown in the
next day and brought to Fisher Funeral Home. The priest
then asked all of us to bow our heads; he lifted Bubba up

in prayer as he placed his hands on C.H. and Francis. After his prayer, the priest moved a chair and sat at the kitchen table with the mourning parents and the aunts. He was offered a sandwich but he kindly refused. Richard and David entered the room and asked for food, which they received and devoured. Warner, Herman, and I were leaning on the kitchen counter. The priest seemed to be most compassionate and loving as he comforted the parents.

The next day C.H. went to the funeral home to finish making arrangements; Bubba's body arrived while C.H. was meeting with the funeral director and C.H. began weeping again after all the details were worked out. The funeral services were held three days later at St. Paul's Catholic Church. Warner, Herman, Donnie, and I were among the pallbearers. The church was crowded and many were in tears. Francis and C.H. were stoic; they had a deep faith which sustained them well.

As the years passed, all of Francis's siblings died. Donnie died, Warner moved, Richard moved, I moved, and David moved. Herman had a wife and children there and he continued living in Vicksburg and was most attentive to Francis and C.H. David after they had returned from college. Eventually I was assigned to preach at a church in Vicksburg and I moved back home from Nashville with my wife and two sons. We were able to visit Francis regularly. I remember my sweet Aunt Francis even at 95 years old tearing up over her son Bubba but it never affected her deep faith. We talked about him often when I returned to Vicksburg and his memory still lingered with us. My wife was also a pastor and Likewise served a church in Vicksburg.

One night we rushed to Francis' house to comfort her after receiving a call that C.H. had passed away after a long, debilitating illness; we waited with her for the undertaker to arrive. We were both with Francis just before she died several years later. My wife softly sang a protestant hymn that Francis had never heard and Francis briefly opened her eyes and looked quizzically at Clare before she lay back and enjoyed the hymn; she never woke up again.

So that was it; the whole wonderful family we had loved so much had crossed the Jordan. They meant so very much to all of us; may God bless them.

photo by Charles E. Rice

Statues of Pain and Negativity

Prelude

My wife and I had been moved to the northeastern part
of our state. We were both ordained ministers and our
churches were not very far apart. I was in the village where
William Faulkner died and she was south of me in a place
called Buck Snort. Her new assignment was adamantly
opposed to having a woman serve as pastor; we were not
informed and went in blind to what she would face. The
issue became readily apparent when her church refused to
pay her moving expenses. Then one thing after another
began to crop up. She had faced these matters before and
as usual just rolled up her sleeves and went to work. Other
places to which she had been assigned had acted similarly
and she had always been able to win them over and serve
successfully, but such was not to be the case this time.

She faced lack of support from her supervisor and
continued complaints from the church. The bishop called
a meeting in which my wife would answer to interrogation
from three supervisors from different districts. The first
meeting was aggressive and hurtful; having done nothing
to warrant such inquisitions, she was dumfounded and
confused. She decided to bring my brother, an attorney,
to the next meeting. She thought that he would be most

supportive and helpful. He was not offered a seat at the meeting and stood silently listening. The male district superintendent who was participating nodded off, but the two female supervisors were aggressive in the attacks on their ordained sister.

Finally, my brother said, "Ladies, I think you are enjoying this just a little bit too much." One of the ladies began to balk and back off but the other became angrier, almost turning grey in her rage. The meeting ended and the decision came several weeks later; my wife was to be removed from the church which she served because she was a female.

Arrival

PSALM 36:1-4

Sin whispers to the wicked, deep within their hearts.
They have no fear of God at all.
In their blind conceit,
they cannot see how wicked they really are.
Everything they say is crooked and deceitful.
They refuse to act wisely or do good.
They lie awake at night, hatching sinful plots.
Their actions are never good.
They make no attempt to turn from evil.

My wife and I were apart for over a year. She moved to New Orleans and began working for a chaplain program in a large hospital. I was still serving up near Memphis and with preaching and visitation was rarely able to travel to see her. She came up every weekend she could, but there were many in which she was on call and could not travel. After a year, I requested of the bishop a location closer to my wife. My supervisor called within days and said most curtly that a church might be available and the bishop would consider transferring me to that place after the necessary meetings and paperwork. People from the village in which I served helped me pack after the decision to send me closer to my wife was made. They were sad to see me depart and I was sad to leave but we understood.

I arrived at the new assignment late in the afternoon with two congregants from my soon-to-be former church who wanted to help me move. No one from the new congregation was there to greet me, and I was stunned to see the former pastor's wife wandering around in the rose bed smelling flowers. I waved at her, but she left without speaking. I sensed that something was amiss. We unpacked the truck and placed my clothes in the parsonage that I would briefly call home.

This was to be my tenth church. I was not worried; all my previous stations had loved and respected my ministry and worked with me. The new church was located on the edge of Honey Island swamp north of Lake Ponchartrain. It was in a small village surrounded by a national wildlife reserve. I began work the next day. Pulling into the pastor's parking spot, I noticed the sign out front that said in bold letters "Open minds, Open hearts, Open doors." My first thought was, I hope so.

The secretary was a massive woman with a cranky disposition; my office was down the hallway from her. She teeter-tottered down to my office early that morning thinking I would be most interested in recent gossip regarding the former pastor and an affair he had supposedly been involved in. Not knowing whether to believe her and not interested at all, I asked her not to mention it again.

My Efforts Begin

PSALM 10: 4-11

The wicked are too proud to seek God
They seem to think that God is dead
Yet they succeed in everything they do
They do not see your punishment awaiting them
They sneer at all their enemies
They think, "Nothing bad will ever happen to us
We will be free of trouble forever."
Their mouths are full of cursing, lies and threats
Trouble and evil are on the tips of their tongues
They lurk in ambush ... waiting to do harm
Like lions crouched in hiding

*They wait to pounce
The wicked think, "God isn't watching us!
He has closed his eyes
And won't even see what we do!"*

I set up my quarterly plan while pondering the ancient oaks outside my new office. Evidently the church was not involved in mission work; everything was or seemed to be about them. So I decided to attempt to involve my new congregation in various missions. We would feed the homeless, provide nourishment for indigent school children who had nothing to eat on weekends and we would attempt to help anyone who came to the church seeking assistance instead of sending them to the police station, which was the previous policy. I planned a series of sermons on spiritual growth in an effort to bring the people on board with me. Before school began that fall several other churches had come on board with us. The only resistance I had up to that point was our treasurer, who complained adamantly about our finances. But even he ceased when we began taking in ample money from the community for the programs. The missions program appeared to have potential for success. I thought that my tenure would go well just like my other assignments, but I was sadly mistaken.

The Pastor Parish Relations Committee fired the secretary early in my appointment. She had insulted a family with a crude joke while they were considering having a wedding in our sanctuary. The choir director was furious after the secretary's dismissal. She stormed into my office thinking that I had instigated the firing without seeking her permission. In addition, her daughter-in-law's joining of the church had been miffed. The daughter-in-law had called me and requested to join, but since the secretary was gone the announcement failed to appear on the weekly bulletin. I forgot to call her forward that next Sunday. At the end of the service, the young lady walked up front and stood with me. I realized what was happening and led her through the ritual of joining the church. The incensed choir director was far from satisfied. The following week, I apologized to the young lady for the error with regard to her joining. In addition, I informed our choir leader that

I had nothing to do with the secretary's firing. It was a decision made by the proper committee and they did not need her permission. My impression was that the musical director did not believe nor forgive me.

Soon after, a lady who was fond of me told me, "They will get you in some form or fashion, believe me. It has happened to every preacher we've ever had here over the past twenty years." She and I both chuckled when I asked if I needed to take a bottle of Kiwi Shoe polish into the pulpit with me, but soon it started.

One man was angry about my sermons on spiritual growth. He demanded, "What is the preacher talking about? Don't preachers do all the spiritual stuff here? What is spiritual growth anyway?" Lack of understanding aside, others turned on me because I had served a glass of wine requested by congregant at dinner in the parsonage one night and because of my testimony in a sermon about my successful bout with alcoholism twenty-five years previous. The choir director came to my office after I had given my pulpit testimony to inform me that the church does not need such honesty from their pastor, especially on the radio. In addition, another lady said that she had been disgusted since day one of my coming because I listed all the sick in prayer and asked God to place them in Christ's white light of protection; her belief was that the white light of protection was heretical and new age. Storm clouds were gathering rapidly.

But we began growing. In fact we were the second fastest growing church in the Sea Shore District. The problem was that the people in power did not like the new folks coming in to our church family. One gentleman entered my office after Holy Communion in which a new member had helped serve and angrily said the he did not want trash serving him the elements of Holy Communion. I replied, "My friend, doesn't our Bible say that we are all sinners?" He aggressively repeated his judgment on the communion server. I smiled and told him that we had no way to impose a DNA test every Sunday and he stormed out of the office infuriated. I felt like I was stuck in the mud with my tires spinning. What could be done to fix the problem?

The Turning

PSALM 22:11, 16-18

Do not stay far from me, for trouble is near,
And no one else can help me.
These people surround me like a pack of dogs;
An evil gang closes in on me.
Spare my precious life from these dogs.
Snatch me from their jaws and from
the horns of these wild oxen.

The centennial year had kicked in and the power structure was now most obvious to me. It was three ladies and one man backed by less than ten others who were supportive but not as active in the power grab. I recognized what was really going on when I walked into the sanctuary one Sunday morning to retrieve a bulletin; the four were having an unannounced meeting there. The group consisted of the choir leader, a banker, and a local attorney and his wife. The lawyer sat placidly chewing his nails as the three ladies' faces meshed in anger. I heard the word preacher mentioned several times. I shuddered; I knew now what I faced. They did not notice me as I picked up my bulletin and left the sanctuary for my Sunday school class.

In spite of these people, the church was growing and thriving. I still had hopes that I could win my antagonists over. I was pleased with the success of our ministries and the dedication of those who were working on them. Many members were fond of me but the conflicts continued to grow. The centennial committee lead by the banker wanted me to preach on the founding of our greater church and the principles on which it was based during the centennial celebration. In the first centennial sermon, I used an analogy by John Wesley in which he told of Christians entering the yard, proceeding to the porch and finally entering the house to receive all the promises offered by the Lord. I followed with a mention of a recent statistical report by George Barna in which he touted that only 15% of the 2.1 billion Christians on earth today actually seek a deeper relationship with the Lord. I Likewise mentioned that 70% of folks in organized Christianity today are not

spiritually inspired or fed because of the politics and power grabs rampant in all denominations. Reminding the congregation that the door of grace and forgiveness remained
open, I stated that too many of us just stand in the yard or
on the porch pouting with our arms folded because things
are not going our way. I reminded them that things should
go Christ's way, not our way, and the only way to enter the
domicile of which Wesley spoke was to submit to Christ.
Leaving the sanctuary that day, the banker lady hissed
in my ear, "You better start practicing what you preach
preacher." I replied, "I'm trying, are you?"

The next day the music director came to my office
and informed me that I was seeking revenge in the pulpit.
She was of the view that the person to whom I referred as
standing and pouting was her lady banker friend. She informed me that she was hiring a bus large enough to take a
hundred of "her" people up to the office of the bishop to
let him know what a wonderful church she had and what
a terrible job I was doing. I was polite but I replied, "First
of all, you can't fill a bus with your supporters; maybe a
mini-van would be big enough. If you really believe I am
seeking revenge in the pulpit then save yourself a trip.
Use my phone to call the bishop and my supervisor. If
your view is correct I don't belong in the pulpit." She was
aghast at my comment and more convinced than ever that
I did not belong in her church. From that point on she
started taking up more and more time with her music and
giving little sermonettes in between songs, which gave me
at times less than 10 minutes for the sermon. I was sad and
depressed about the situation facing me.

Several months later, the youth minister, embroiled
in the same toxins, resigned in tears. She had done an
excellent job and the youth loved her but the power
structure did not; she could not take anymore abuse. In
fact many of the folks who diligently ran the various
ministries would not come to church because of the
conflicts which continued to grow. The day after the youth
pastor resigned the banker stopped me in the hallway
behind the sanctuary before the service and told me not to
mention the resignation. I replied that I had not planned
to mention... She interrupted, "I'm serious. This is my
church Preacher!" I replied softly, "You are wrong; this is

Christ's church." Whirling around, she almost broke the high heel off her shoe and stormed out of the church. I was told later that she listened to the sermon on her car radio to be sure I did not mention anything with regard to the youth pastor in the pulpit.

After that, I was not on any of the centennial committees nor was I informed of the meetings. The following Sunday I preached about feeding the homeless, disagreement in the church family, and the Trustee's decision to disband our ministry dealing with mentally challenged adults. No names were mentioned; I merely asked for those who disagreed with me to show me in the Holy Scripture where it says do not feed the homeless. In addition, bring Scripture, not political essays, to discuss if you happen to disagree with something I have said, adding, "Would Christ have cut off the mentally challenged as we just did?" Several folks leaving growled at me when they left the sanctuary after the services but I would not have compromised anything I said that day.

The following Tuesday we had a Pastor Parish Relations Committee meeting; the meeting was mundane and uneventful. Following the meeting, I returned to my office to get my car keys and my brief case. The chair of the committee followed me to the office, knocked and said that everyone on the committee had gone except one member who wanted to speak to me. We walked back to the meeting room where the lawyer's wife was waiting. Her face was twisted with a scowl; she began yelling almost immediately about my sermon the Sunday previous. In all honesty, none of what she said in the tirade made any sense at all. I listened and repeatedly asked that she lower her voice because she was disrespecting her pastor. Finally, after 45 minutes to an hour I had had enough. I told her I had an idea. She stared at me with steely eyes. I said, "How about this solution: I get up every Sunday morning about 5:30 a.m. and seek God's guidance on the sermon; why not let God sleep and I'll just call you and ask you what to say?" She became even more infused with anger and got up to leave the room. The committee chair hissed, "Preacher, you have crossed the line!" I replied, "Am I the only person in this room who has done so?"

Later that night another congregant called me and

said that she had seen a massive angel standing beside the pulpit during the previous Sunday service protecting me. I was not surprised because I had prayed for the first time that Sunday for protection in the pulpit. The protecting angel brought comfort but I was up to my neck in negativity and toxins and I was exhausted and getting ill. I decided to consult with a spiritual director for help; I knew what was coming. My spiritual advisor told me that I was under attack and that my health was threatened. Her advice was, "Leave this church as fast as you can. You can't change it."

Beginning of the End

PSALM 4: 2

How long will you people ruin my reputation?
How long will you make groundless accusations?
How long will you continue your lies?

PSALM 17: 9-12

Protect me from wicked people who attack me,
from murderous enemies who surround me.
they are without pity. Listen to their boasting!
They track me down and surround me,
Watching for the chance
to throw me to the ground.
They are like hungry carnivores
eager to tear me apart,
waiting and hiding in ambush.

The lawyer's wife who had yelled at me was now talking about the necessity of my departure to whomever would listen. She cornered a group in the choir one Sunday and went on and on about the need for my removal. Wearily, one lady finally asked, "What has he done? I love him very much." The angry woman replied, "It is best that you don't know what the preacher has done!" In essence the door had been left open for anyone to imagine any number of terrible actions on my part. Word spread all over the church.

The lawyer's wife then took over the vital planning committee, which was an open committee with no chair and decided to expand and change the directory that had been reduced for reasons of expense. In addition, the committee, with only five attending, requested that I be removed as chair of the worship committee. Their desire was to place the virulent attorney in charge of worship. Shortly after the meeting, the lawyer's wife and the musical director walked into my office. They informed me about their decided changes to the directory and my tenure as chair of the worship committee. I replied that I was against changing the directory because of cost and the fact that people weren't going to read it. But, I would check the discipline regarding a congregant being in charge of the worship committee. Leaving my office, the lawyer's wife turned to me and growled in her usual manner, "I am going to change the directory like God wants me to; I'm not going to hell! If they don't want to read it then they can go to hell!" I was beyond stunned at the shallow level of her belief that the church directory was indeed the key to heaven and hell. I knew that my days were numbered, and I felt a heaviness in my chest.

That night in a dream I found myself standing on a sandbar on the river of God's living water. I noticed a vessel with my antagonists on board going upriver against the current. I watched them curiously; they seemed to be making no progress at all. They were attempting to head up stream against the current of God with ultimate self-confidence and massive egos. I watched them sadly; their craft was making no progress whatsoever. The lawyer and his wife occupied the pilot house and were gleefully guiding the ship. The banker was proudly strutting up and down the deck and the music director was on her cellphone attempting to reach the Celestial Choir. A small group of less than ten were on board as well. They were the powerbrokers' supporters who had remained in the background for the most part. I bowed my head in prayer for all of them. After the prayer, I wondered what motivated them. Perhaps they were deeply scarred and had cut themselves off from the saving wellspring of life. Maybe they thought that religion should bless the status quo in which they were deeply immersed, or that the purpose of church was to make them feel good. I wondered most sadly whether they realized that they were concocting a cheap grace which allowed them to feel good about themselves without confronting their sin. Almost everyone on the craft had adamantly informed me that they did not come to church to hear about the painful issues in our society; they wanted to leave church feeling good. The notion of escapism was prominent in their thinking. Such a focus helped them avoid the difficult struggle of contemporary living. Religion for them was not concerned with the broken world; it was concerned with life in another place. Therefore the difficult teachings in our Scripture need not be taken too seriously.

Waking the next morning, I was more aware than ever that I was facing a hill that would probably prove to be insurmountable. I knew that the people in the church for the past two decades were not focused on the teachings of the Lord; holiness was absent. Of course any church in existence has a group who are blinded to the Holy in their midst. Many of us, like them, have embarked on a course that is most difficult from which to detach. We separate ourselves from the holiness and depth of life itself. Today we reside in an infertile field; we seek our life in shopping, beautiful cars, power, and money. But we are not the first culture to do so. Over the centuries brave souls who genuinely saw the truth tried to integrate that truth into the church's belief system. They were not praised or honored for their efforts; in fact, many were persecuted. Any clergyperson today who does not take Kiwi shoe polish into the pulpit and speaks forthrightly on this matter will feel the ground shaking and trembling beneath his or her pulpit. Ministers are most vulnerable today, and that almost forces us to make our sermons comfy or we will lose our job. The people want to assume that they are living Godly lives and if their preacher says anything contrary his days are numbered. We live in a time in which many desire that preachers stick to happy, clappy stuff and not utter the deep and wonderful truth of the Lord. Such a path of keeping Christ's true teachings on the backburner and not mentioning anything that numerous members feel is radical makes our religion convenient and comfortable and allows us to hide from God.

Several days later the centennial committee had finished the history room and wanted me to come tour it. My picture was on the wall in the room and I asked why I was in the history room. They informed me that I was already part of the archives. Everybody in the room roared with laughter. I left the room in sadness.

In the midst of these pejorative events the centennial celebration finally arrived. The banker praised her family, who sat proudly in the first three rows, for founding the church. No doubt about it, it was their day. Obviously my tenure was nearly over.

Palm Sunday was my last day. I announced that I was seriously ill. I had been diagnosed with squamous cell carcinoma located in my mediastinum and I had filed for medical leave and had been approved. After the sermon, titled "More than a Parade," I walked down to the alter rail as usual and bowed my head in prayer. The choir director thought that the choir would do the one song and then I would be ushered out as finished for good. Taking charge yet again, she approached the mike and asked my wife to come down and stand with me. She had no idea that she had opened the door to a spontaneous demonstration by those numerous people in the congregation who supported and loved us. They continued to come up weeping and hugging my wife and me during the hymn of invitation. Those who did not want me there sat petulantly in their seats as the crowd descended upon us. They gradually became aware that many congregants were looking at them. Realizing that they were being watched, the choir director and the lawyer's wife came up and lavished hypocritical words upon us. The banker and the lawyer had left the sanctuary almost immediately, knowing that their job was done. Then everyone held hands and circled around us to offer prayer for my healing and our future. Before I closed my eyes for the prayer, I noticed that the choir director and the lawyer's wife who had come up to appease the congregation had refused to join the prayer circle and were already on their way out the back door headed for lunch. I left town later that afternoon.

A New Beginning

JOHN 8:32 & 36

God is the real, created the real and is with us now.
Of that we can be sure.
But whether he created the religious dogma
or not is another question.
The real will set us free, and we shall be free indeed.

PSALM 43: 1-3

Declare me innocent, O God!
Defend me against these ungodly people
Rescue me from these unjust liars
For you are God, my only safe haven
Why have you tossed me aside?
Why must I wander around in grief?
Oppressed by my enemies?

Send our your light and your truth;
Let them guide me.
Let them lead me to your Holy Mountain
the place where you live.

PSALM 18: 16-19

He reached down from Heaven and rescued me;
He drew me out of deep waters.
He rescued me from my powerful enemies
From those who hated me
and were too strong for me;
They attacked me at a moment
when I was in distress.
But the Lord supported me.
He led me to a place of safety.

Rejected, my career was at an end and I was seriously ill. I had been swimming in a toxic river and had been weakened and hurt. Gradually my thoughts strengthened as I turned to the Lord; I was not banging my head against the wall crying "why me." I believed that this was the opportunity for a new beginning. I accepted that there was a deeper meaning to this situation and that the Almighty would help me. I started treatment; I was involved in radiation, chemo, and Reiki. My physical treatment focused on daily radiation and weekly chemo; the primary treatment for beyond the physical realm was Reiki. One church member, incensed at my having Reiki, called me and fussed. He referred to me as a "so-called Christian" and asked how any believer could submit to Reiki treatment. I asked him to show me in the Bible where Jesus mentioned chemo and radiation. He took the usual path of my antagonists and slammed the phone down immediately.

Soon after, I was blessed with several inspirational visions during prayer and meditation. I found myself on a sandbar in a river. I recognized relatives of mine who had already crossed the Jordan and I was most glad to see them but I was upset at the appearance that I was joining them on the other side. They ignored my fear and after greeting me placed me on my back in the river. I floated down river looking up at the night sky. I was at peace and happy. Every now and then I would turn and swim or go underwater and come back up and rest on my back. Suddenly my journey was interrupted by noise on either bank. I could hear screams, gunfire, shouts of anger, then flashes of fire and light. In short, just what humanity was now embroiled in all over our broken world. But I knew that I was in God's peace and could stay there in his living water and if I had to go on shore he would be with me. I was blessed.

Several nights later I was awakened from slumber standing at the foot of a flight of stairs. Angels stood on either side of the stairway. Christ appeared at the head of the stairs. I had never visually seen the Lord before and not knowing what else to do I fell on my face in the dirt. Someone lifted me and stood me up straight and dusted me off. Christ walked down the steps and touched me on my chest. Since then I have had no pain and my tumor has shrunken substantially. In addition, my spirits have lifted increasingly higher and higher. I began praying that I would continue a deep and lasting spiritual journey and that I would be in total submission to the Lord. I realized that such was the only place to be.

The following week I was having trouble sleeping and was tossing and turning. Before I knew what was happening, angels were escorting me up another short flight of stairs. They placed me on a funeral pyre and lit the fire. At first I cringed, expecting great pain—but I felt no heat. The angels communicated that what was being burned away was my vanity, my pride, and my ego. They were removing all the earthly things that I, like many others, had so often depended upon. Then I was assisted back down the stairs to a stone bench. I sat on the bench exhausted, empty, and spent. Before I could gather my thoughts the Holy Spirit filled my body, my aura, and my chakras with its eternal light and I rested in glory and peace. The next morning a Christian psychic for whom my wife had worked in New York City called and said that she had been shown that the tumor was no longer existent on the ethereal level and that I would be healed.

My New Life

PSALM 30: 1-3

I will exalt you, Lord, for you rescued me
You refused to let my enemies
Triumph over me.
I cried out to you for help,
you restored my health.
You brought me up from the grave,
O Lord. You kept me from falling into
the pit of death.

Sick and worried and out of a job I had loved, I prayed for God to remove any and all negativity within me with no reversal on me or anyone else. I knew that healing

was more than mere physical results, and I was seeking
all levels of healing: mental, emotional, and physical.
In response to my prayers, I seemed clear of any and
all negativity for several days. It was almost as if I was
standing in a beautiful newly mowed field of green grass
on a spring day. Then suddenly visions of statues of past
hurt and pain appeared in multitude; they came as statues
of granite and marble. I recognized them; in fact, I had
been dealing with them for most of my life. I had provided
space for them for many years, figuratively furnishing rent,
lights, and air. I had tied my identity to them, but somehow
I realized that I would not heal with these incidents still
influencing me and my view of myself. They promoted a
false self, not the real self that God had created, and they
kept me locked in a container from which I desperately
needed to emerge.

I knew that they must be dealt with, so I cautiously
proceeded in prayer and meditation to the dark and
desolate street in my hometown where these monuments
of pain and negativity resided. The street was down near
the river in the warehouse district. The atmosphere was
sinister and threatening with empty buildings and very
little light. The narrow street was covered with trash
and abandoned vehicles. As I walked, the old buildings,
unmarked and unnumbered, hovered over me. It was as
if I was being watched by unseen demons; they seemed
to be observing me through the broken windows of
the warehouses. I continued fearfully to the building
housing my statues of pain and heartbreak. The door was
unlocked; I entered the building.

I jumped back surprised and frightened. A figure
dressed in a white robe and holding a lantern with
three candles greeted me. He smiled and said that I was
expected. I was stunned and shocked to see someone in
the building. Looking at the figure, I felt like I had known
him somewhere, but I could not think of when or where.
I soon relaxed and was trusting and comfortable with
his presence. He asked me to sit and talk with him for a
moment. He said that my willingness to come here gave
to me the opportunity to disengage my identity from the
horrific experiences I had faced and to make space in
my soul to see the Divine at work in my life and in the

world. Continuing, he told me that negative experiences tend to become prisons where we can be shackled and trapped for a lifetime. Over time we can have little sense of self beyond our negative experiences. We are not able to develop a sense of self beyond the experience; we see ourselves as no more than the event itself. We are what happened to us and nothing else. But these experiences never tell us who we really are; they do not define us. A false self is created when we link with the experiences and the shackles are locked. He said that change can only come when we begin to grasp a concept of a grace-filled, loving God who yearns to be connected with us. This ability to see and claim the Divine within us and move out of the negative experience is the key to moving on. We can be freed in this manner, when we intentionally let go of the pain and experience ourselves as being more than the end result of a series of events. Thus we can begin to experience our identity apart from our horrific experience, and we begin to create spiritual space in which we begin to see and claim the presence of God. We can begin to think in terms of original blessing rather than original curse. Blessings then come and the true self that God created in us can emerge.

I knew then that this robed figure was my spirit guide; he was a representative of the Almighty and I knew that was just what I needed. He continued, mentioning that a well-known human scholar, Carl Jung, said that the sole purpose of human existence is to kindle a light in the darkness of mere being. Another wise human, Joseph Campbell, responded to a question about humans going on our journey not to save the world but to save ourselves. Mr. Campbell's response was that the answer was not in our salvation but in our submitting to our Lord and not relying on our false selves. The world without spirit is a wasteland. The majority of people have a notion of saving the world by shifting things around, changing the rules, establishing institutions. But the only way to bring life to the world is to become alive yourself in the Lord. My guide then stated through a smile, "That, my friend, is why we are here today."

He then stood and held his hand out to me while he told me, "We live in the fullness of God's time, not earth

time. In God's time your real self can begin to emerge.
I am aware of your past. I know that you have suffered
much, but when you quit drinking twenty-five years ago
and submitted to counseling you made much progress. I
am aware that you were a pastor and that you have had
numerous positive experiences with the Divine; you have
become connected in many ways. God's seed is within
you; the very cells of your body are longing and yearning
for the Almighty and his healing presence. I would ask
you then to kneel and pray for forgiveness before we tour
the granite and marble statues of your pain. As a former
pastor, you know that confession of your sin involves
an objective change in your relationship with God and a
subjective change within you. It is a vital part of your healing and the transforming of your inner being as you turn
from the false self to the real self. Remember healing will
be incomplete if you get trapped in anger; holding onto
anger delays the movement toward forgiveness and letting
go. You must trust God and ask for his love and grace in
your healing. When you pray remember that you are held
in the palm of God's hand and called by your name. You
are precious in God's sight. To refuse God's forgiveness,
as many do, and remain bound by neurotic guilt leads to
depression and a suppressed immune system, which leads
to illness." I complied and knelt in prayer of confession
and repentance.

The spirit guide reached and helped me up after the
prayer. He looked me directly in my eyes and said, "Before
we enter and view these statues of pain and heartbreak,
let us have a brief discussion of healing. Healing reveals
God's nature and is a sign that his reign has already broken
forth into the present. So your job is to submit totally to
the Lord and let your false self and your identification
with these experiences fall away. Acts of healing defeat the
powers of darkness and evil; healing brings wholeness, not
perfection. It means you will be escorted into completion,
into spiritual maturity and wholeness. Such is God's desire
for you and everyone and his love for us gives us all a
center to that which is fragmented by our illusory self." As
the spirit guide opened the massive door to the granite and
marble statues of pain and heartbreak, he made one more
comment, telling me that I had lived in isolation and that

my partially healed wounds propped up an illusory image of myself. This tour should and would be healing and life changing. "God be with you!"

We entered the first room through a massive mirror. My image was that of a small child. The spirit guide did not project any image. We entered and stood near three monuments of my early wounds. For the first time I noticed how bright the spirit guide's three candles were and I wondered if they represented the Father, the Son, and the Holy Spirit. The guide held his candles up over the first statute. "What is this?" he asked.

I replied, "It is my grandmother boarding a train after an argument with my mother the day before I was born. We did not see each other again until I was nearly 10 years old."

Moving to the next one, he said, "These are connected aren't they?

"Yes," I replied. "My mom and I were arguing about her giving me another bottle of milk."

"I sense that you aren't terribly upset about these, are you?"

Thinking for a moment, I replied, "No. Both of these women had negativity imposed upon them and I have prayed for them to be released and healed."

Moving to the next monument he held his candle up and said, "What is this?"

"It was in the front yard of an apartment house where we lived, and a child in the Hicks family hit me in the head with a horse shoe. But it was my fault because I had snuck away from Miss Roberta, who was watching me."

My guide laughed. "Let's keep moving then."

We entered another area of statues. My spirit guide asked, "What is this circle of boys around you?"

I looked down sadly. "It started here. We left the apartment house and moved to a neighborhood called Glenwood Circle. From the moment we moved into the neighborhood they came after me. That day these neighborhood boys would not let me out of the circle that they had formed and they kept pushing me back in as I tried to escape. Several of them were teens and all of them were much older than me. After I got home, I told my mother what had happened and she screamed angrily at me, 'Just fight them.' I was confused and not comforted because I was unsure how to fight any boy so much older than I was."

The spirit guide asked, "Are you deeply bothered by any of these Glenwood incidents?"

"No, I'm basically over them. But in some way I remained linked to them and in that way they have influenced me greatly."

"Isn't there another problem here?"

I responded, "Yes, I never understood why they chose me, or what was or is it about my DNA that led to this. Why me? Why not choose another kid?"

The guide raised his lantern and asked, "Is the next monument connected?"

"Yes, one of the boys in the circle that day locked me in his closet several months later and would not let me out."

Moving down and holding his lantern up, he said, "And what about this one?"

"My next door neighbor's oldest son hit me in the eye with a hoe and came close to putting my eye out. The next one is an occasion where a boy who I thought was my best friend came after me with another boy and pelted my dog and me with rocks to make us leave his yard."

We then came to another mirror and my image was of an older child; again no image for my guide. We entered through the mirror and stood silently, then we approached the first statue. My guide held his lantern high. It was me as a third grader most embarrassed because of a stammer which had developed. I was in reading class and had been called upon to read and couldn't finish. The teacher was calling on another student because of the time I was taking up. "How are you with this one?" asked the guide.

"I'm okay. Stuttering affected me until late in my twenties and even ruined a career plan, but I am over it now. I've had much counseling with regard to this problem."

The spirit guide smiled. "What's the next one?"

I sighed. "I'm on my back porch. I had tried out for little league baseball and had not received a call to be on any team. It was the second year I had tried out and was not chosen by any team and I was crying in disappointment."

"How are you with this?"

I laughed. "Well, I played on the so-called farm team. My little brother thought I planted baseballs but I made the all-star team all three years I played in the farm league. I'm alright now."

My guide continued. "What is this monument of you standing with a bag over your head?"

"Well, I began to isolate and withdraw. I had big goals and none of them were working out. I had few close friends because I had turned on myself and was thinking 'why bother?'."

My guide paused and examined the next statue. "Looks like you are in college in these next ones, but we have no mirror to go through because you in many ways were still a child. This statue has you sitting in a pile of unopened books. You look sad and depressed. What about it?"

I frowned. "Well, I was a lonely failure. My father's fraternity did not offer me a bid and my grades plummeted. I left after one semester and went to the Institute of Logaoedics for speech therapy. I felt like I was earmarked as disabled. The next monument is of me graduating from college. Any pain you see my face is because my family was not there."

"What's this next one of you in uniform?"

I thoughtfully replied, "I came home and worked for a relative's business and was not happy. So, as you see in the next statue, I went to law school in an attempt to be like my father. The scene you see is of me in class after being called on to explain a legal issue. My stammering response sounded like a recording of a car that wouldn't start. I took up the last ten minutes of the class with my verbal hemming and hawing."

"One more room to tour, but what is your view of these after you have done this part of the tour?" asked the spirit guide.

I thought and replied, "I'm tired of thinking about them and bored. For the most part I think I am over these incidents and I have no anger against anyone involved. In fact, some of it was my fault. In my mind I have grown past these issues, with God's help. My stammer and stutter is now cured, I have made peace through prayer with my mother and grandmother, and education-wise I have a doctorate degree. The only issue I have is that I let these issues become my identity."

The spirit guide responded, "I understand, but thank our Lord for your perseverance which gave you traction and hope for this day. Now, let's tour the last room."

We entered through the last mirror and my image was of an adult; again no image for my spirit guide. We stop at the first monument of my wife with her hands tied behind her back and people circling her and holding their fists in the air with twisted scowls on their faces. My wife's statue stood with eyes closed as if in prayer. The bishop and three district supervisors stood in the background smiling and doing nothing. The guide asked, "What happened here?"

I replied sadly, "Well, my wife was in a church that did not want a woman pastor, and they came after her and had her removed from the pulpit. She got no support at all from the church hierarchy."

"How is she now?" inquired my guide.

I looked up at the statue. "She is thriving. She just got her doctorate and she serves as a hospital chaplain."

My guide looked me in the eyes and asked, "What is the last monument?"

I stated sadly, "It is the end of my career."

"What do you mean?" he inquired.

"Less than ten persons in a church of over 250 people were able to run me off and make me ill with constant attacks. Can't you see me standing there surrounded by a small circle of people with contorted faces and a complicit large group in the background? I loved most of them but I refused to compromise God's truth like they wanted and I would not shine their shoes and make them happy."

We stood at the end of the row of statues. My spirit guide put his lantern on the shelf and said, "What a blessing for you to have toured these monuments of pain and negativity. Don't misunderstand. You don't have to forget these events; they happened to you. But, the time has come to release the false identity based on these events of pain and heartbreak. Don't be lulled into thinking that these events were not horrific. In addition, don't incorrectly think that to move beyond these events negates the importance of them. What happened to you formed the crucible in which your psychological, physical, and spiritual being developed. Your task is to recognize and honor the presence of the Loving God in your life and in your being. The caring energy has always been with you and is with you still; God's power resides not in force or condemnation but in love. Remember, disengage from the events and be grounded in awareness of the Divine; such allows you to return and look at these events with clarity and compassion. These events happened to you but they do not define who you are and they never will."

We walked silently towards the door. The robed figure stopped and put his hand on my shoulder. He smiled at me and said that a new paradigm had emerged. A renewed fullness of life is now possible through communion with the Holy Spirit of God. The process is never completed, but the implications are radical indeed and blessings will abound. Your identity is now beyond the crucibles of these events; this is now a museum. Open these windows and let the Divine light shine into all corners. He handed me the key to the building. We hugged and continued towards the back door. I felt complete and full of joy. I remembered the passage in 1st COR 13, "when I was a child, I spoke as a child, understood as a child, I thought as a child but when I became a man, I put away childish things."

I closed the door and locked it and turned to face my guide but he had disappeared and was high in the night sky as a shining light.

Sunbelt

I don't have any idea how long we had been following the truck, but if you squinted into the noon glare the familiar pig's head logo could be made out with the words "Portion Control Meats, Good Taste for Good Times." I felt no pride in the fact that the vehicle was from Mr. Sunbelt's own massive fleet. He had a long day in front of him and was sleeping soundly in the back, so I decided not to wake him to tell him we were behind one of his trucks. The old man was also asleep, nodding fitfully in the sun with his banjo beside him.

Over the past twenty years the old man, Sunshine, and I had made many of these trips from Old Dominion to New Iberia; it was all usually connected to one of Sunbelt's schemes. The old man came to remind us, and I just drove.

I could smell the salt in the air for about an hour before the gulf was visible. We dropped Mr. Sunbelt and his scissors off at the ribbon cutting ceremony. The old man and I used stay in the early days and laugh about how every time Sunbelt cut a ribbon his accent was two or three inches shorter, but the joke wasn't funny anymore.

This day I followed the dimly scrawled map that led us to Beauvoir, the Jeff Davis death house. A fire helped ward off the chill from the sea. The old man stared at the house all night, as each tired plunk of his banjo marked the withering and browning of some magnolia blossom deep in his dreams. As for me, I looked out at the barrier islands and wondered if I was strong enough to swim there.

The two of us left early the next morning; Mr. Sunbelt could find his own way home.

www.ingramcontent.com/pod-product-compliance
Lightning Source LLC
Chambersburg PA
CBHW050742250626
47155CB00005B/1890

*9 7 8 0 9 9 7 1 6 9 5 3 9 *